Murder at Mass Rock
by Penny Johnston

Penny Johnston, Publisher

Penny Johnston, Publisher

The characters and events in this book are fictitious. Any similarity to real persons, living or dead, is coincidental and not intended by the author.

ISBN: 978 0 99 3997945

Cover Design by Sara Carrick

Detective and Mystery stories, Canadian (English). Johnston, Penny

Other Mariposa Murder Mysteries by Penny Johnston

Therapy for the Dead (2015)

Frozen lies the Librarian (2016)

Dedicated to the late Lillian Uren, Richard and Wendy Johnston

Acknowledgements

Thank you to Alex Wilmot, editing; Sara Carrick, design and art work; Robert Barnett, photo.

Penny Johnston

Prologue

The night was dark. The moon was hidden behind clouds. A strong wind rustled the tree branches. An owl hooted from a distance. A tall figure in a black cowl, with sandals on his bare feet and carrying a heavy, black bag slipped through the trees, silently and furtively heading west towards the stream.

Not far behind, silent figures with cloaks covering their faces hurried along, carrying candles and torches to light the way, following the hooded figure through the woods.

At the stream the leader put his bag down, pulled his cowl from his face and crossed himself in front of a large rock with a flat ledge. Then he took out of his bag a chalice, a cup, candles and a cross.

If caught by Cromwell's soldiers holding an outdoor mass, everyone present would be murdered. The priest's body, dead or alive would be worth twenty pounds to the soldiers, who were on a campaign to wipe out the Irish Catholics. For nine months, Cromwell's army of English soldiers had invaded Ireland (1649-1650).

Chapter 1

Clancy sat down at his desk. Greg was sitting in his chair firing paperclips into the waste paper basket. Clancy shouted, "Get hold of yourself, Greg. Have some discipline."

"I have been thinking about the latest break in. I have been meditating."

"Do it silently then."

The phone rang. Clancy picked it up. "Hello," said a deep, cultivated voice, "is this Clancy Murphy?"

"Yes, who is calling?"

"Let me introduce myself," the cultivated voice said. "My name is Eli Brown, of Eli Brown and Associates. Our law offices are located at Eglinton and Avenue Road, here in Toronto."

Clancy had heard of him before. The law practice had a high profile in the media for handling, estate cases that ran into thousands of dollars when litigated. He could picture his office, soft leather chairs and sofa, large mahogany desk with a heavy glass paperweight, Mont Blanc pens, wall to wall bookcases with leather bound books, Canadian Law, several luscious secretaries in mini skirts ready to bend over at a moment's notice, classy and expensive. Whereas when he looked around his Mariposa office, it was Salvation Army rejects, wobbly slanted chairs that were hard to sit in, dented filing cabinets, coffee cup stains on the wooden desk, uneven drawers that never closed, stuffed with files and memos that said important. It was IKEA at its worst.

"My client is the late Ms. Mary Murphy, a third cousin of yours who met her unfortunate demise a few days ago in Toronto.

"She passed on, did she? We weren't close. She was part of

9

the other branch of the family and went her separate way. We exchanged cards at Christmas and that was the extent of our relationship. Why are you calling?"

"Your cousin," he continued, "I am sorry to say, met an untimely death. She was murdered."

"That's not good news. When did this happen?

"Several days ago. I was contacted by the police as I am her lawyer, her executor for her estate. As her personal lawyer and the person who drew up her will, the police wanted to know to whom she left her money. Maybe somebody bumped her off to get their hands on her money. It might provide a motive for someone wanting to murder her."

"Your phone call is the first I have heard of it. I am not her heir, nor would she make me her heir. Why are you calling me? What do you want me from me?"

"The reason I called you is that she left a codicil in her will. You are not the main beneficiary but are mentioned in her codicil. She has left you a nice sum of money. I should also inform you that she was in the sex trade, she was a prostitute even though she was in her early seventies. She was very discreet about her private life."

"She was a prostitute! That's news to me, I don't think any members of the family knew that. You say she left me a sum of money? Wow! That's grand of her. But why me? What amount are we talking about?"

"$50.000."

He whistled, "that's a nice amount of change. But what is the stipulation. Are there are strings attached, they're always is. Do I have to rob a bank to get it? I hope it's nothing illegal."

Mr. Brown laughed. "No, but it involves travel back to the old country to the Murphy seat in Cork for a visit. There is required a minimum stay of two weeks. After you have done that you can collect."

"What do I do on my visit?"

"That's up to you. Squire Murphy is head of the clan and has a manor house outside of Cork, the second largest city in Ireland. He has a large farm. Ireland is a beautiful country to visit. The time will fly by and soon it will be time to come home. Have you been there before?"

"Never, but my ancestors came from there long ago. After the potato famine, the family split in two. Our side came out. Many of us perished of typhus on the voyage out 45 days at sea, in 1856. But here I am. What will I do there? Twiddle my thumbs?"

"Some suggestions. Whatever strikes your fancy. I have the name and address of Squire Sean Murphy, as your contact. Perhaps that would be a good place to start by writing him and telling him you're coming. Drop in and see the squire. I know he would love to have visitors from Canada. Inquire after the family genealogy, visit the neighbours, have lunch in Cork, go to the pubs, etc. Stay a minimum of two weeks, then your obligation is complete."

"How is the police murder investigation into her murder going?"

"Early days yet."

"It's a strange request but I will honour it. I need to take some time off, I have some time coming to me. Two weeks should do the trick."

"Then it's settled. Let me know how you got on. You know our address send me a Xerox copy of your return ticket to Ireland and we can start the probate for the will."

***

Clancy whistled at his desk. The sun was shining, the sky was a beautiful blue. Today is my lucky day. I've won the lottery. "Greg," he shouted over to him. "I've got good news for me and bad news for you. First the good news. I am going on leave as soon as I can. One of my relatives has passed on."

Greg was hunched over a binder of reports of break and enter, trying to see if there was a pattern in the time of day and mode of entry. There were so many different ways and no pattern. Try as he might he couldn't find one. He needed a cup of coffee.

"What's up? You're looking too happy about that. That is not good news, a death in the family."

"The death in the family was someone I hardly knew, talked to or saw. A distant relative. In fact, she didn't just die, she was murdered."

"That is worse, still not good news."

"Don't look at me like that. Unknown to me, she was in the sex trade. Maybe a client bumped her off. We don't know for sure at this point. The case is ongoing."

"My, my, a relative of yours was in the sex trade. I thought all your relations were on the up and up? Nuns and priests? Wasn't your uncle a priest? That must have been a bit of a shock to you to find out that she was a sex trade worker."

"Well it did give me a jolt when I first heard about it, but then we just exchanged cards at Christmas. We weren't close. I hadn't a clue as to what she was up to in Toronto. They get up to all sorts of things in Toronto.

"Now I am getting to the good news. Her lawyer, Eli Brown contacted me from Toronto to tell me that in her will, in a codicil, she left me $50,000, on one condition. The stipulation is that I take a trip to Ireland to get involved with my roots, the Murphy clan who have an ancestral home near Cork."

"Did I hear you mention, money? You were left money?" asked Greg incredulously. "You can afford to pay for the coffee and doughnuts from here on in."

"Oh, don't be like that. Jealousy is not a good thing to have. I will bring you back a souvenir from Ireland, maybe a four-leaf clover. How about that?

"Why she left it to me, I don't know. A crazy whim of hers and I hardly knew her. But I have always been interested in history and the Murphy clan, my ancestors will probably turn out to be murderers and sheep stealers."

"I didn't know you still had relatives in Ireland."

"Neither did I. Apparently way back in the 1800s, in 1847 during the great potato famine in Ireland when the crops didn't mature, and the potatoes rotted in the field and no one had anything to eat, there were two brothers. One of the brothers came out with thousands of others on those coffin sailing ships as they were called because so many of them died in their bunks, down in the galleys at sea from typhus, a louse found in their clothing. A bite was deadly. It took them 45 days on a sailing ship to reach Grosse Ile the quarantine station in the St. Lawrence River, about two hours by water from Quebec City.

"Most of the Irish rode in steerage in the hull of the boat because they were poor. The conditions on the ships were horrible, filthy food, lack of water and typhus. Over 5,000 perished at sea from typhus and over 3,000 perished in the hospitals on Grosse Ile once they got here. Even then when the ship was cleared of the sick, everywhere the ship docked after Quebec City, typhus spread.

"His family were lucky, most were spared. Only one died, the wife. She is buried in the Irish Cemetery at Gross Ile. Her name is on the glass memorial at Grosse Ile, now a national historic park.

"After a decent interval, he married again which is natural. He had young children to raise. Those immigrants who survived farmed along the St. Lawrence River then as time went on, travelled down to Montreal and some established themselves on farms in

Ontario. As good Catholics, they had big families. *Be fruitful and multiply*.

"So, this cousin of mine who was murdered is part of the Murphy clan. There are so many of us that we all seem to have gone our separate ways. It's hard to know everybody."

"When are you going?"

"As soon as the paperwork is done, and I talk to my old lady, Agnes. She will be glad to get rid of me for a couple of weeks. Greg, I want you to keep an eye on things in the office.

"I have some time coming to me and I thought I would take two weeks off, go over and have a look around, meet some of the clan, and come home, a nice simple excursion and then collect the money. It will be a nice change.

"On the internet I will find a cheap flight to Dublin and then take the train down to Cork and from there take a taxi out to the ancestral home. Aer Lingus has direct flights from Toronto to Dublin."

"Why not Air Transat? You want to take a charter, it's cheaper. But flying coach, you're cramped like a herd of cattle into a small space. Try to fly business class or get an upgrade. I guess you don't have any points to trade in?"

"I think I will splurge and fly business. It is an 8-hour flight and me legs could get cramped. I do like the drinks they serve, and I am not going to worry about getting dehydrated or developing deep vein thrombosis in the back of my knees. Yeah, a nice seat all the way.

"Now to dust off my suitcase, tell the little woman, where I'm going, put in a request for leave and then be off. I'll write to the squire, at the address that her lawyer gave me, to let him know that I'm coming."

"Yeah, sounds like a good idea. $50,000 is nothing to sniff at. David and I can handle things until you get back."

"Oh sure", thought Clancy.

***

Agnes had been out shopping and he had to wait until she came home with the groceries. He helped her put them into the cupboard. Finished he asked Agnes to sit down in a chair, he had important news to tell her. "Agnes, I have got some great news. A relative has passed on and she has left me $50,000 on condition I visit Ireland for two weeks.

"What fairy story are you telling me?" said Agnes, not believing a word he had said.

"It's the truth, Agnes. I will be gone for only two weeks. Ms. Mary Murphy left a codicil in her will requesting that I visit the Murphy seat in Cork. When I have done that, the money is all mine."

"Two weeks is a long time to be gone," said Agnes plaintively.

"That is the condition of the request and I can't help that. I can be back before you know that I have gone. I have asked at the office to go and they have approved my leave."

"Well," said Agnes," I am not too happy about it just the same. "

"I had better start packing." He headed upstairs to the bedroom and got his grip down from the closet shelf.

First, he put in four pairs of clean underwear which his mother had always told him to wear in case of an accident. Then five vests, socks, and a couple of sweaters. He packed after-shave lotion. The hell with the 'No scents means good sense crowd', with their allergies. Toothpaste, brush, hairbrush, bandages. No, there would be a pharmacy over there and he could buy anything he needed.

Agnes with a stony face stood by and watched. She was not too pleased.

Several days later, he kissed her goodbye, then got into the hired limo to take the trip down to Pearson International to catch the overnight Air Lingus flight to Dublin. Once inside the limo, any stress that he had felt in his job went out the window. He was on holiday.

***

At the Aer Lingus check in desk, for business, he didn't have to wait in line. His luggage was immediately tagged for Dublin. He was ready to go through customs and board. Once on the plane, he took off his leather jacket and stowed it in the overhead bin then settled into his roomy seat. He decided to enjoy himself. How often could he afford Business Class? Not often. Never. This was a real treat.

He had done all the things he was told by his doctor not to do. He had been told to wear support hose in case of deep vein thrombosis. The hell with that. Support hose, only old ladies wore them.

Aer Lingus was soon above the clouds. He watched the path

of the plane on his screen. First one hour up to Montreal then up along the path of the St. Lawrence River to the Gaspe then across Newfoundland and then to the bottom of Greenland. It seemed like a long way to take. Until he remembered that the earth was round, and the plane was following the curvature of the earth. A lovely Irish Colleen was pushing the drink cart, what he had been waiting for.

"Champagne as we lift off?" she smiled at him.

"Great," said Clancy.

A few minutes later it was, "Martini or cocktail?"

"A bloody Mary," said Clancy getting into the spirit of things.

"What will you have for dinner with your meal? We have a wide choice of wine available. "

Now isn't this the greatest, thought Clancy.

Who cares about dehydration. He accepted all the offers of any free liquor the Colleen had offered him even the after-dinner liquors Why not? He was on vacation.

He'd been told by his doctor that you're supposed to get up and walk every hour to prevent deep vein thrombosis. But he was happy just to sit as he was in his comfortable seat in Business Class, away from the crying babies in coach, who would squall all the way to Dublin.

He noticed that, in the next seat, a man in his forties who looked like a government official, was shuffling papers into his briefcase. He had his laptop out and was looking for a place to plug it in.

"Working holiday?"

"I have to go to Dublin on Canadian government business, to issue visas for young Irish Immigrants who want to come and work in Canada. We're looking for people in the trades to work in construction. We have quite a shortage. So, it will be all work for me there except for a drink in the local pub at night."

"Well, for me," said Clancy, "it will be all play. I am going to look up the Murphy clan in Cork County."

"Ah, Cork is a beautiful city. They unfortunately have lots of unemployment like the rest of Ireland. That's where we get our immigrants. Ireland is a beautiful country. The people there are so friendly. Ever been there before?"

"No, but my ancestors came from Ireland. Murphy is my last name. I don't believe in leprechauns or the wee people. Do you?"

"No", he laughed. "Got to do some paper work before we land. It's been nice talking to you."

"Sure thing," said Clancy, "I would never want to get in the way of someone working for a living."

Chapter 2

There was a bit of tail wind but otherwise the flight to Dublin continued smoothly. Time passes quickly when you have had a lot to drink.

When the plane touched down in Dublin, he staggered off. Clancy had jet lag. How he ever got through customs he didn't know. What had he to declare? Not like Oscar Wilde who claimed, 'only my genius'. 'Nothing' was as good an answer as they would get from him. Once through customs, it was the fast speed train ride from Dublin to Cork which had been a blur. He couldn't even remember purchasing a ticket or how much it cost. Did he still have his wallet in his rear pocket? He patted it to make sure. He hoped his passport was safe somewhere.

Outside the Cork Railway Station, he hailed a cab and snoozed through most of the ride to the Manor House in the back of the cab. "How much farther down the road do we have to go?" Clancy asked the taxi driver.

"Just a hop and a skip. It lies behind the hedgerows."

Clancy looked out the window. For miles he could see only barns, farmhouses and farmland, and then to the right he spotted something familiar. "There's a pub. The Crossroads. Stop here and let me out. I need some refreshment to take the chill off the day before I pop into the manor. Thanks, my good man. Keep the change." Clancy hopped out

The cab driver shouted as he drove off, "Enjoy your stay. Kiss the Blarney Stone for me."

"Not likely," muttered Clancy under his breath. He stood for a moment surveying his surroundings. Acres and acres of rich green farmland stretched before him, marked off by grey stone dykes, hedges and rows of trees. The pub with its thatched roof had a large outdoor parking lot, with picnic tables out in front for those who wanted to drink outdoors. Smoke was coming out of its chimney.

This is a good idea, thought Clancy. Don't want to be blundering in. Test the waters first. See first what the locals have to say.

He didn't have to walk far, just a few steps up to the front door of The Crossroads which was flung open. He ducked his head, entering a low beamed room, with a fire in the grate and a farmer standing in Wellington boots at the bar sipping a pint. The pub looked like it had just opened. The farmer was the only one there. On the bulletin board on the wall was posted a notice for a Celtic musical evening, on the next Saturday, with fiddlers, tambourines and drums. That sounded interesting.

"*Caed mile failte.* A hundred thousand welcomes. You are only a stranger once in here. Set yourself down, make yourself comfortable in front of our peat moss fire. What will you have?" The bartender, a middle-aged man wearing a big apron, leaned over the bar with a big smile on his face. "My name is Liam Cross. I am the owner and manager here."

Clancy nodded "What does everyone here drink?"

"A pint of Guinness."

"Why not." said Clancy

He watched the gnarled hands pull on the handle

"Is that an American accent?"

"No, I am Canadian."

"My apologies. I can't tell the difference between the two."

"I won't hold it against you."

The middle-aged farmer who was standing by the fire, looked up at him quizzically. "What brings you to these parts, if I may ask?"

"I've come to see the old family estate. Not staying that long. Maybe two weeks at the most. By the way, my name is Clancy Murphy."

"Ah, then you must be related to the country squire down the road."

"A poor relation, I'm afraid. There was a family feud and it ended with our side immigrating. The feud and the potato famine did us in. We would have starved if we had stayed. I just thought I would knock back a pint before bumping into the squire."

"He's a bit of a toff. Not friendly like. Does not mix with the locals. Doesn't come down to drink here with the other farmers.

Keeps to himself, more so since his wife died. Don't expect a warm welcome there. Since the accident, he has gotten his nephew Edward to do the work that Seamus use to do on his farm. Edward's brother, the youngest one, Quincy, is a lazy lad. He doesn't do much, drink and watch TV. Useless.

"Don't mind me asking. What kind of work do you do? There's not much work in these parts. Unemployment is high and most of the young have immigrated to Canada or Australia. Don't blame them there is nothing for them here."

"I am a police officer back in Canada. Right now, I'm on vacation."

"Are you now? A member of the Gardai which is what they are called over here. You might be interested in the mysterious death of Seamus Murphy, a nephew of the squire. It has never been properly resolved."

"Like I say, I am on vacation. I only have a short time here."

"Too bad. Drop in here anytime it gets a bit chilly up at the house. There's always someone to talk to down here. Are you staying there?"

"I am not sure yet where I am staying."

"There's a room we let over the pub, if you want to stay here," said Liam

"I will keep that in mind. Good day."

Well fortified with Dutch courage, Clancy stepped onto the road. The same taxi driver, who had been waiting for him around the corner of the pub, pulled up.

"How did you get on? On your way to the manor house? I am going that way. Hop in," and Clancy did.

Chapter 3

"You couldn't miss the manor house. It stands out for miles," said the cab driver appreciatively, as he slowed down so that Clancy could get a good view.

The countryside, of rolling hills and dales, spread out before him. Small stone cottages with grey slate roofs dotted the landscape. Sheep were everywhere.

In the midst stood a large Palladian style villa with a circular, gravel drive leading up to a massive front door. It had no turrets or towers but was several stories high, with a great portico over the front door.

It was very impressive thought Clancy, too rich for my blood but he got a secret thrill out of visiting the country seat of the Murphy clan just the same. The taxi driver drove up the driveway and let him off at the front door.

What to do next? There wasn't a buzzer, so Clancy raised the brass knocker on the massive oak door, but the door swung open as he did so. A man in a black morning suit stood there waiting.

"Are you Squire Murphy?" asked Clancy

"No, I'm Mansbridge, the butler. Will you come this way? Let me take your luggage." Clancy stepped into the Great Hall. A knight from the Middle Ages, in steel armor holding a sword and shield, greeted him. On the walls, oil paintings in gilded frames ran the length of the room. Everywhere he could see heavy antique chairs lined up against the walls. Heavy silk damask curtains from floor to ceiling draped the stain glass windows. He felt like he had stepped back in time, into Downton Abbey or even earlier.

"Squire Murphy is expecting you. I have lit a nice fire lit

especially for you in the grate. Have you come all the way from Canada?" asked the butler. "My, my. I have relatives in Toronto, I haven't seen them in years. They have their life and I have mine. Come this way."

He led Clancy through the Great Hall to the library, where a roaring fire was going in the massive stone fireplace, above which hung the Murphy family coat of arms. Around the room were portraits in gilt frames of former heirs. Clancy presumed they were the previous Murphy owners of this manor and estate. On the wall opposite the fireplace, was a floor to ceiling tapestry of a knight on horseback holding a javelin, followed by a pack of hounds.

Squire Murphy was standing in front of the fire warming his hands. He was a tall man, much taller than Clancy had expected with big hands and big feet. Dressed in a black velour jacket with satin collar, and black pressed wool trousers he looked every inch the country squire.

"Miserable day out isn't it? There's a lot of rain in these parts. That's why our grass is so green. Can I offer you a glass of sherry, Clancy? Call me Sean. Sweet or dry? We should be on a first name basis since we are cousins." He indicated a large leather chair on the other side facing the fireplace to sit in. A reading lamp stood beside the chair.

Clancy thought it would be rude to say no after drinking a pint of Guinness. But would sherry mix well with beer? He didn't think so but, oh well, he was on vacation. "Yes, thank you."

"Let's sit down here by the fire and keep ourselves warm" said the squire pulling up another chair." I will put another peat log on the flames.

"I am delighted that you wrote and told me you were coming to see me. Was your trip tiring? It's a long journey from Canada. I hope that the plane ride was not too unpleasant. How was the food? So, so?"

"Not too bad I rode in Business Class. Treated myself this time, instead of being wedged into a seat in economy like a herd of cattle."

"I got your letter and I was very pleased to know I had a relative in Mariposa. Until you wrote, I didn't know I had one."

"Ms. Murphy's lawyer, Eli Brown of Toronto, gave me your address. He is handling the estate."

"I am glad that he did that. Ms. Murphy has visited us in the past. Dreadful, that she was murdered. Have they caught the person yet?"

"Not that I am aware of."

"My wife died a few years back and I am alone in the house. If you like we could put you up during your stay here in Ireland. It would be no problem, no trouble at all. My housekeeper will be only too happy to get your bed ready. It gets lonely in these parts."

"Are you sure I wouldn't be putting you out?"

"Not at all, then it's settled. I will invite another member of the clan, Hugh Murphy, my brother, to come over and visit. He had three sons, until the accident which I will tell you about. He said he might drop in tomorrow. Hr lives on a neighbouring farm. He wants to see his Canadian connection. I will phone him this evening and check that everything is suitable. Are you agreeable?"

"I hope it is not too much trouble."

"No trouble at all."

"What would you like to drink with your dinner? Not so long ago we had hardly any Irish wineries, but now we have quite a few in Country Cork. We weren't then known for our wine making. One wine, Lusca is made in Lusk, the north county of Dublin. In my cellar I have a nice chardonnay, a cabernet or a merlot. It is your choice, Clancy. Or a nice rich, burgundy wine, good for circulation."

"You make the choice," said Clancy, "I am not very good at choosing."

"Very well, let it be my surprise. After that you can put your feet up before dinner. My housekeeper will take your suitcase upstairs."

A quick drink then Clancy was ready to put his feet up.

Clancy followed Mina up the grand stair case to his bedroom.

The room was large with a with a four-poster bed with a side table with a reading lamp on each side of the bed and an electric clock. At the foot of the bed was a cedar chest for holding wool blankets. On the opposite side of the room was a large stone fireplace.

***

Having dinner with the squire was an occasion straight out of the movies. There were so many forks on the table beside his china plate he didn't know which one to choose from. "Start from the outside and work your way in should do the trick," he thought.

There were a couple of crystal goblets, one for water the other for wine. Which was which? Mansbridge made that decision by pouring water into the nearest goblet.

To start off the meal, there was a green salad placed in a china bowl There was a pause, then the roast was brought in on a large platter. Mansbridge stood beside the squire and carved.

"How do you like it? Rare, medium rare, or well done?"

"Well done."

Mansbridge lopped the beef off onto his plate. "a little gravy?"

Everything was so delicious and served with style. Clancy thought he was eating in a five-star restaurant, with a candle-lit candelabra in the centre of the table. The Squire was at one end of the long oak table and Clancy at the other end. Instead of passing the food, Mansbridge brought the dishes to him

Dessert was pudding, a nice rich sweet chocolate, loaded with calories.

The Squire didn't say much at dinner and Clancy was glad of that. He was tired from his trip. After dinner, Mina, the house-keeper, took Clancy up the long winding staircase to his room at the front of the house whose window overlooked the countryside

Mina turned down the coverlet, plumped the pillows and then went over to the fireplace and lit a fire. "It should give enough warmth to the room before you turn in. Would you like me to get you a hot water bottle and put it in your bed? It gets damp in the evening."

"No, thank you. That won't be necessary."

"Put out your shoes when you retire and Mansbridge will give them a nice polish. Have a good sleep. You must be tired after your long flight," she said, and closed the door behind her.

Suffering from jet lag, Clancy fell immediately into a deep sleep. He slept soundly under the quilted coverlet until, the noise of the window frame banging against the wall awakened him. The latch had been blown open by the wind and he had to get up to close it. The smell of wood, smoke and wet leaves made him even more wide awake. In the distance he heard a dog howling out in the field somewhere. There was a full moon, but he could see nothing beyond the trees. Another dog began barking below. Then he heard the sound of heavy, slippered footsteps coming across the wooden floor towards his door. Slowly the door handle turned. He froze. Was someone trying to break in? An Intruder? Should he go stand behind the door? He was defenseless. His heart skipped. He had left his gun back in his locker in Mariposa. The only weapon he had was his flashlight. He grabbed it and held it ready. Then the footsteps stopped. He waited, his hand ready to smash down with the flashlight as soon as the door opened. The footsteps receded. He waited for a few minutes, then hearing nothing more, he went back to bed but not before propping a chair under the door handle just in case whoever it was came back.

The next morning, he went downstairs for breakfast. The Squire was there already, reading the Cork Independent. The fire was lit in the grate.

"Did you have a good sleep?" asked Squire Murphy.

"Like a log." Clancy decided not to mention about what he had heard in the night, in case it had been a dream caused by his long flight and jet lag.

"That's good. Hugh Murphy, my brother, will be coming over for morning coffee. Help yourself. It's all laid out on the sideboard."

Clancy chose a boiled egg, some toast, marmalade, some cheese. Then he went back and brought a cup of coffee to the table.

"Well, we had an unusual death in the family about two years ago. I had become very fond of Seamus, my nephew, Hugh's boy. He took the place of a son around here helping me with the farm, the sheep— shearing them, taking them out to the field. There are a lot of chores to do around here. I miss him a great deal. As I've no children, Seamus being the eldest of Hugh's sons, was going to be left my estate when I die. But now that's not possible. Hugh has two other sons, Edward and Quincy. Quincy is unstable, he never sticks to anything. I'm trying out Edward but he's not too enthusiastic about what he has to do around here. I pay good wages. I'm fair. But that's the way it goes.

"Seamus was a good-looking lad, very helpful and so obliging. One morning he told me he was going to take the tractor and a wagon to the woodlot, load up on wood and bring it all back in the wagon. I waved him goodbye and off he went.

"He didn't come back for lunch, which he usually does. I assumed he had brought his own lunch or gone back to his father's farm to eat. I thought nothing of it. Then in the afternoon I began to get apprehensive. I expected him back for tea, which he always enjoyed, but he didn't come.

"I drove out to the woodlot and found him. It looked like he had tripped or fallen under the tractor, and it had pinned him down, crushed him to death.

"I called emergency. The ambulance got here, and they performed CPR, but he was long dead. The coroner came out to assess the situation. Not many get run over by their tractor, especially someone as capable as Seamus.

"There was a couple of strange things that I noticed. The key was turned off in the ignition and the gate to the fence was swinging wide open. I could see tire marks in the muddy ground, beside the tractor tracks. Someone must have been visiting, but to this day I don't know who.

"Ms. Murphy, our cousin in Canada, the one that got murdered, had been fond of him and corresponded with him. She flew over for the funeral. He had phoned her at Christmas and Easter. He informed her of the local gossip, kept her up to date on things that were happening in the area. I imagine she would have left him money in her will if he had lived.

"We had a service in the little parish church, down at the crossroads. Most of the locals came, the pub owners, the farmers, the tradesmen. During the service there wasn't a dry eye in the place. Seamus was a pretty popular fellow and popular with the girls, a good-looking man, with his jet black curly hair and deep blue eyes.

"Afterwards, we carried the coffin back to the manor. I had the most room here and could accommodate everyone for the wake. Ms. Murphy who had flown over for the funeral, drank herself silly, not a pleasant sight. She was slurring her words and dripping the ash from her cigarette over everybody's clothes. She told everyone how she had loved Seamus like a son.

"The parish priest, Father Flynn, was not much better. He drank his whisky like a fish and was stumbling around muttering, 'tis a sad day for Ireland when a young man dies,' giving sympathetic pats on the back, telling everyone to brace up, and then peering down the young women's dresses.

"Today, with Hugh, we will drive out to the spot where Seamus died."

***

Promptly, at ten, there was a knock at the door and Hugh Murphy, in a heavy knit Aran sweater, cloth cap and black leather breeches was ushered into the room by the butler. His cheeks were rosy from the wind and the cold. Clancy judged that he was close to the same age as the Squire.

"We'd lost contact with our Canadian relatives. I didn't know we had any but am pleased to find that we have." said Hugh, holding out his hand to shake Clancy's.

"Yes, it was a surprise to me too. Our cousin, Ms. Murphy who was unfortunately murdered left me something in her will on condition that I visit the Murphy clan in Ireland. That's why I'm here.

"I can't tell you much about her. She kept to herself although we didn't live too far apart, about one and half hour drive from Mariposa. Why did she make that stipulation in her will? I don't know. We weren't close. We exchanged greetings every year at Christmas and that was about it. I guess she knew I was a policeman. I was shocked when I received word from her lawyer that I was the next of kin. She was my third cousin. Perhaps you can help me with that question?"

"You're a member of the Gardai right? A policeman? Well you heard what she did part time which might explain why she kept her distance? We didn't know until we read about it in the paper," said Hugh.

Clancy nodded. "She was a sex worker which really shocked me. This I found out d after she was murdered."

"No one in the family had any idea that she was into that not even Sean although he corresponded with her. Maybe she wanted you to look into something."

"You got that right about being a policeman, but I'm on vacation, no sleuthing about." Clancy laughed at his joke.

"Have they any idea who the murderer might be?" asked Hugh.

"Early days yet. My best guess is that it was one of her clients. She booked them over the phone. Perhaps, one of them turned nasty. That's my best guess at this point."

"'I told Hugh," said the Squire interrupting "that we would go on a tour of my property in the car, including down by the wood-lot, and see where Seamus had his accident. It might interest Clancy, being a policeman and all. This might be what our cousin wanted him to look into while he's over here."

"The fresh air will do us good. Work up an appetite for lunch," said Clancy.

The farmlands sprawled over several hundred hectares, a patchwork quilt of rolling countryside. Some fields lay fallow, while others were covered in hay stubble. Dry stone walls divided the fields. In one field, cows were grazing on grass and clover. Everywhere there were sheep. A few goats nibbled at the base of a tree. In another field, several horses were walking next to the fence

27

that held them in. Beyond that was the moor consisting of peat, pink heather and bracken, dotted with occasional yew and prickly yellow gorse. Before they got into the car, the Squire went over to pat one of the horses, Nellie, he called her, then got back into the car

"Grouse and pheasants roam in the fields surrounding the woodlot," said the Squire, pointing.

They made their way down the winding road that led to the centre field. Just beyond was the woodlot.

"That's where it happened, just over there. A sad day for all of us."

"It broke my heart," said Hugh. "I still don't understand how it could happen and there were no witnesses."

"What time of day?" asked Clancy, his curiosity aroused.

"Late morning, we think. The coroner could only specify within a couple of hours."

"There is the spot where it all happened."

The men got out of the car and looked around. Clancy was struck by the beauty of the countryside, the varying shades of green and yellow fields, the small forest of oak, maple and birch trees against the blueness of the sky. He looked down at the ground, but it was just a mass of tire tracks, indistinguishable from each other, with weeds, sedges and moss everywhere you looked. They got back into the car and returned to the Manor for lunch.

The housekeeper had laid out the lunch, buffet style with pickles, pickled eggs, meat pies, bread, lots of cheese and plenty to drink.

After lunch, when Hughes had left for home, the Squire said, "I will show you the clippings that I kept from the newspaper about the accident. Here, you can read them at your leisure."

Clancy thanked him and took the clippings into the library and turned on a lamp. *Local Farm Lad run over by tractor*, and his picture.

The accounts were very similar to what the Squire had told him. The coroner had ruled it an accidental death. There had been no inquest so there had been no questions about the cause of death. No one had spoken of any concerns or problems with the conclusion. "Mm," thought Clancy," not much to go on. Maybe this was why his murdered cousin who had been very fond of her nephew, had left him money in the will, to come over to Ireland to take a look at things, to take an interest in this case. Who knows?

"Nap time," thought Clancy his stomach was so full he thought it might burst. He excused himself to the Squire and went upstairs. He was enjoying every moment at the Manor. He loved being waited on.

When he rejoined the Squire in the lounge after a leisurely nap, he announced his plan to do a little sightseeing.

"I think tomorrow I'll go over to Blarney Castle and kiss the Blarney stone."

"Don't do that. It's a tourist trap. There will be hoards of buses and tourists surrounding the place," advised the Squire.

"Well I would like to see it anyway, maybe not kiss the stone. Just to say that I've been there. Back home everyone will ask, if I went there."

"In that case, I will drive you over. It's just 8 kilometres from here, five minutes by car. On the way I'll point out a Mass Rock which is an interesting sight. During the 1680s to the 1700s, known as the Penal era, the British under Cromwell forbade Catholics to practice mass worship. Priests were often hunted down and murdered, but they did it anyway. This had to be done secretly, in places which were hidden from view. So huge rocks with flat ledges were found in the countryside in small glens and forests, on which to celebrate mass. Some are now on private land, some hidden in forests, some by streams. One such rock had a holy well beside it which became known as warts well, for the healing of warts. All had a flat ledge for communion cups and places to stand candles. They were known as Carraig an Aifrinn, or Holy Rock. The one at Blarney has the profile of a priest's face etched on the stone face. We can find it on the R519 route.

"Then we'll go to Blarney, a granite stone castle covered with moss which sits atop a hill, very visible to all. It, in itself, is not that interesting. To kiss the blarney stone, you lie on your back on the stone floor. A cranky old man will lift you belly up through an opening in the walls of the battlements to kiss the stone. It used to be more dangerous, but safeguards have been installed. Then the visitor was held by his ankles and dangled down to the stone.

"It's most unsanitary, with the tourist leaving lots of lipstick and spittle on the stone which feels pretty wet and slimy. The thought of catching a disease puts me off. That's why I advise against it. I've never kissed it, nor suffered from want of the gift of the gab.

"Besides, it might prove difficult to hold onto, you being a hefty figure. No, I am joking, grills have been placed in the wall as a safety measure," said the Squire laughing.

They drove over. The scene was exactly as the squire

predicted. Hundreds of tourists like lemmings scrambled up the grassy knoll to the castle's ramparts.

"Do you want to walk around?" asked the Squire.

"Yes, an overview would suit me fine. Too bad I didn't bring my camera."

"Another place not to bother with is Killarney. It's full of tour buses, and streets lined with Holiday Inns, and outlet malls. The locals will do anything for a euro. It's a shame. The tourists don't get to experience the real Ireland. But the Ring of Kerry, a gorgeous vista, is not to be missed, with its mountains, lakes and the ocean."

They walked around the ramparts for a few minutes getting wonderful views of the countryside below, of farms and cottages in all directions. Clancy spied a patch of clover and kneeled down to look for a shamrock. As luck would have it, he found one. He opened his wallet and pressed it amongst the plastic for safe keeping. They got back into the car to return to the Manor House. Coming around a corner another car coming from the opposite direction came out of nowhere. It almost ran them down. The Squire steered quickly into the nearby hedge while the other car raced by. Back on the road, Clancy heaved a sigh of relief. "That was a close call. Did you get a look at the driver?

"No. The car was going too fast."

"It's too bad we didn't get the license number. We could have phoned it in for dangerous driving."

Chapter 4

Clancy was spinning his wheels sitting in the library before lunch. The Squire's dog had fallen asleep on the hearth. In the grate, the fire had gone out. On the table, the Squire had left a message that he had to go out to the barn to check on things. Mansbridge had gone to do some chores elsewhere in the house. Mina, the housekeeper, was making the beds and tidying the rooms upstairs.

Now, with no one around and no one to listen in on his conversation, would be a good time thought Clancy, to put into a call to the office. There was a five-hour difference between Ireland and Canada. He wanted to see how they were getting on without him. Things would be in chaos. They'd be begging for him to get back. He could picture Greg eating an apple and aiming the core for the wastebasket, missing it.

He recognized Greg's voice at once. "Greg, it's me, Clancy."

"Who?" said Greg, "I didn't quite catch that."

"It's me, Clancy. Who did you think it was? Justin Trudeau? How's it going? Miss me?"

"Miss you? Like a dog needs a bone to chew on. Nothing's happening here. The usual. No excitement. Just the odd break and enter. One old lady claimed that she was sexually assaulted by a man in her bed at the Sunshine for Seniors Centre. Elder abuse, got to stop that I thought. I went up to investigate and heard her story, but she was very confused. Each time she told the story she gave me a different description of her attacker. First, she described a male attendant with a moustache as having done it, then it was the cook who had a beard. She couldn't get her story straight. After the interview, as I was preparing to leave, an administrative assistant quietly took me aside and told me she had early dementia and not to believe a word she said. Why hadn't she told me that at the first place? All that time I wasted listening to her cock and bull stories." He paused to take a breath.

"The weather is terrible, raining non-stop but what can you expect in the fall? Every other day this particular old lady comes in and wants to use our toilet on her way to the bank or to go grocery shopping. She tells me it's an emergency. After she's left I go into the toilet to check that everything is left neat and tidy and what do I find? Big puddles on the floor. I have to mop up afterwards. What a filthy job. I'm fed up."

"Don't let her in. Lock the door. Say the toilet is busted. Use any excuse," said Clancy. "By the way have you heard anything about how the investigation is going into my cousin's murder?"

"Early days yet. Forensics swept the apartment for finger-prints and found the victim's and several unknown prints, probably clients. None of the prints was in the police data bank except hers for prostitution so there were no matches. The conclusion is that the person who did this, is a first-time offender, which will make it even more difficult to solve."

"I see."

"I think they had a security camera on the front door in the lobby and also on the rear exit, so that might be helpful. If I hear of anything I'll let you know. Anything happening on your end? How's it going?"

"Sleep in late, have breakfast, walk down to the pub, nothing too challenging. The air is so fresh out in the countryside that I could fall asleep during the day in the blink of an eye.

"I'll talk to you again when I have more to tell you. Bye for now." He didn't feel at all needed. Not too much was happening on the home front. Let Greg muddle through everything as he usually did. Everything is a muddle there anyway.

***

After a ploughman's lunch of cheese, bread and pickles laid out at the long buffet table in the dining room, Clancy went upstairs to his bedroom to get forty winks. Then, well rested, he decided to head down to The Crossroads. He left word with Mansbridge where he was going.

On the road outside the manor house, a middle age farmer was coming towards him with a flock of sheep spread out over the entire road, so he couldn't pass. Clancy held up his hands helplessly.

The farmer whistled to his Border Collie and the dog began barking and guiding the sheep over to one side of the road clearing a path for Clancy. "Sheep seem to have the right of way over here," he thought.

At The Crossroads, Clancy felt very relaxed. He didn't have to be on his best behavior like he did up at the manor House. It was a large pub with several chimneys on its thatched roof belching smoke. Inside the low beamed room, the floor was carpeted, and several tables and chairs were scattered throughout. A large fireplace dominated one wall and various country scenes were pictured on brass plates mounted on the wall circling the room. Liam Cross waved him over to the bar.

"How are they treating you at the manor? When you didn't come back here, I figured you were going to stay the night there. A bit grand, eh? Set yourself down and make yourself comfortable among us peasants here."

"Fine so far," said Clancy. "We went out on a nice little excursion over to Blarney Caste, but we didn't kiss the stone. It was a nice drive in the countryside. Then on the way home we almost got sideswiped by a car. Didn't see it coming. The woman who was driving it drove like a maniac."

"That's strange for these parts. Most people drive on the country roads, with their bends and twists, as slow as molasses. It's hard to see over the hedgerows and damn dangerous if you aren't careful."

Liam handed Clancy his pint. A voice at his right elbow asked Clancy, "Your accent? Are you an American?"

Clancy looked over. A small man, taller than a leprechaun, but just, was standing there. He had a shock of black hair, blue eyes and ruddy cheeks. There was a fierce intelligence in those eyes. He was wearing a black wool suit. Obviously, he was not a farmer.

"No, Canadian."

"Sorry for the mistake. No hard feelings. I'm Doc Flannery," and he extended his hand.

Clancy felt the softness of his fingers. Obviously, he didn't do manual work.

"I should know better. After medical school I went out to Canada to do my internship at the Sir Wilfred Grenfell Mission in Newfoundland. The hospital was located at St. Anthony's. Been there?"

"No, I haven't."

"It's interesting. A fishing village on the west coast, not far

33

from L'Anse aux Meadows on the northwest peninsula of Newfoundland. One thousand years ago, a Norse expedition from Greenland settled there. It's now a national historic site. They came long before Christopher Columbus found the new world. Today, the village is recreated with sod huts and preserved mounds similar to 1,000 years ago. A museum there exhibits shards of pottery that have been dug up.

"St. Anthony, where I worked, supplied me with an apartment and I got my meals at the hospital. It is a small fishing village with not that much to do. We saw a lot of cases of patients coming to the clinic with genital itching, burning and discharge. Over fifty per cent of the village was infected with a sexually transmitted disease, Chlamydia, which is treatable and easily curable if caught early enough. Isn't that amazing that such a high number of the villagers would contract that? I guess there was time on their hands to get up to mischief. Not much else to do. TV wasn't enough for them.

"I enjoyed myself thoroughly that year and it was a good experience. Then I returned to Ireland to practice, first in Dublin and now outside of Cork. I hope you enjoy your stay here. What's your occupation?"

"I'm a policeman, but I'm on vacation."

"Ah, a member of the Gardai. Very peace loving around here. Quiet."

"I'm glad to hear that. As mentioned, I'm on vacation and just want to sit back and enjoy myself."

"I'm sure you will. This is a grand pub to do that in."

"How's the Squire treating you?" asked Liam. "Is he cold and standoffish?"

"Not so far. He's been very generous. I'm a lucky man to be staying there. I have the run of the manor so to speak."

"We'll drink to that," said Liam. "but you're welcome to stay here anytime it gets rough up there."

Chapter 5

The fire was out in the library when Clancy looked in. The Squire was nowhere to be found, so he decided to do a little reading in a big easy arm chair, by the fireplace. There was nothing like the warmth from a fire for comfort. He walked over to the bookshelves and found, after reading several titles, a thin book, privately published, detailing the genealogy of the Murphy clan, the family tree; who was related to whom, going back several generations. He settled in the chair to read. Mansbridge the butler came in with a large glass of sherry.

"Sir, to keep the chill off."

"I'm all for that," Clancy said, taking the glass off the tray. "I love being spoiled."

A short while later, the Squire abruptly entered the room looking tired and put out.

"Sorry about my absence but someone, probably some youths, for a prank left the gate open, letting loose the pigs from their pen. We had a hell of a time rounding them up. It was nothing serious, just time wasted in getting them back into the enclosure."

"When do you think it happened? Has this happened before?"

"Probably happened when we were away at Blarney Castle this morning. In the past we've had the odd incident, annoying but not a worry."

"Sounds like somebody local?"

"Could be. Have you enjoyed yourself so far?"

"Nipped down to the local. Met Doc Flannery."

"Oh yes, he's been our family doctor for years, likes to slip into the pub and have a nip 'to keep the arteries flowing' according

35

to him.

"Mina is getting a nice dinner ready for us, roast pork, with mint sauce, roast potatoes, applesauce and broccoli, all the trimmings. I'm going down to the wine cellar to get a nice bottle of wine for us to drink."

"Sounds good. Just reading up on the Murphy clan. Our history goes back a long way."

"Yes, it's a proud lineage that we are part of and I hope it continues that way."

***

The grandfather clock in the corner chimed seven o'clock.

Mina, the housekeeper, came into the room and rang the dinner bell. "Dinner is ready."

They ate at the long banquet table, under the candlelit silver candelabra. The Squire didn't talk much at dinner, his mind seemed far away. Clancy, taking the hint, concentrated on eating the meal, which he found delicious. Afterwards, he excused himself and retired to his room for an early night.

He closed his eyes and was soon fast asleep. He slipped in and out of a dream in which he was a country squire riding a horse in a fox hunt. He rode through the countryside, over the hills and dales, stopping to rest at a farm where they sold apple cider.

It was a nice, comforting dream until he was wakened by the sound of footsteps creaking on the floor boards in the hall outside his door. He looked at the clock on his bedside table. Four o'clock in the morning.

Clancy carefully slipped out of bed and tiptoed over to stand behind the door to listen. The footsteps stopped close to his door then slowly faded away again. He waited to hear what would happen next before going back to bed. Suddenly, he heard a crash below and someone moaning. He rushed out the door and, looking down, saw a large figure sprawled at the bottom step of the stairs.

It was the Squire.

"Clancy, it's you. Thank gawd. Help. Be careful, my foot caught on something and I fell. My ankle's hurting really badly."

Clancy went down the stairs and helped the Squire hang onto the balcony for support.

"Ring for Mansbridge. My ankle or leg may be broken. I can't walk. I can't move for the pain," he moaned.

Mansbridge came quickly in his grey dressing gown and

slippers. They bent down and lifted the Squire up. "We can't get you back upstairs, too much weight. We will have to get you a stretcher to do that. In the meantime, you'll have to stay here.

"Lean on my shoulder and put your arm around my neck and your other arm around Clancy's neck and we'll get you into the lounge where there's a nice sofa to lie down on. I'll get a fire going in the grate. Then I will ring for Doc Flannery to come."

"Oh, don't get him until the morning. Don't bother him in the middle of the night. I can last until then." said the Squire in a plaintive voice.

"Put your ankle up on the sofa and we can apply ice to it. Ice on, ice off will do the trick and rest, lots of rest. RICE is what we say in Canada," said Clancy.

"Thanks so much. Sorry to be so much trouble." The Squire lifted his head up weakly." I heard a noise outside my bedroom, Clancy and I got up to investigate. The sound was coming from downstairs, so I went downstairs to find out what it was. That's when I fell."

After breakfast, Doc Flannery arrived in his red Volkswagen, and was quickly ushered into the lounge where a pale faced Squire was lying on the sofa, his leg propped up by cushions. Doc Flannery carefully lifted the comforter. The Squire's ankle was red and swollen. "I would suggest an X-ray when you're up to it. But," he said, fingering gently the swollen tissue, "I don't think it's broken. You're doing the right thing applying ice. This will keep the swelling down. You'll need lots of rest though, to let it heal. Keep off your feet."

Mansbridge appeared and asked Doc Flannery if he would like some hot coffee, or would a glass of sherry do?"

"Sherry would be fine."

Clancy's curiosity was piqued. He decided to look around, to go back to the front hall stairs and see what had made the Squire trip. He started at the bottom step. Further up the stairs, he found a very thin nylon thread something like a fishing wire. It would be hard to notice if you weren't looking for it. He held the thread and followed it behind the stairs. It had been tied to a nail on one of the spindles and there was an empty nail on the other side. Someone had tried to kill the Squire by making him fall down the stairs. Someone had wanted him dead. His fall was no accident.

This discovery was very disturbing to Clancy. He hadn't been here long enough to know who were the Squire's enemies. "Proceed cautiously" he told himself, "just watch and observe, be a fly on the wall."

Chapter 6

Clancy pushed his chair away from the breakfast table, after having several cups of coffee and slices of toast with mulberry jam, then picked up some extra slices of toast which he slipped into his jacket pocket. First, he was going out to the pond in the field at the side of the manor house to feed the ducks, then he would go down to the pub.

Several mallards were swimming in a circle around the big pond. He stopped to watch then opened the gate and headed for the little stone bridge that spanned one end of the pond. He didn't want to get his shoes wet and ruin the leather. There were tall bulrushes and water lilies growing in the wetlands surrounding the pond. He paused in the middle of the bridge and looked down at the water. So peaceful he thought. He reached into his jacket pocket and threw bits of crumbs one at a time onto the water's surface, waiting for them to be snapped up.

A nice fat mallard male, brightly plumed, quickly seized the bread in its beak and swam off. Then another duck snapped at the bread. He emptied his pockets. "That's all," he said to the ducks who had gathered below him to seize the remainders. He wondered if the Squire would have duck on the menu for dinner some night while he was there? So far, they had had roast beef and pork. Maybe duck would be next.

Now, down to the pub to go over it all in his mind, to think about what had been happening at the manor house.

He opened the door of the pub. A dart thrown by a young farmer whizzed by narrowly missing him. "Got you," said the farmer as the dart landed in the bull's eye.

"Easy does it with that dart," said Clancy. "Don't you think the dart board is in the wrong place next to the front door?"

"No. It's been there for years. Why change it now? Want to play?" the lad asked Clancy with a friendly smile.

"My arm isn't working too well, a little arthritis." This was a lie. "I'd rather sit and watch."

"A lot of people have arthritis in these parts, mostly because of the rain. Sorry you can't join me."

Clancy found a place by the fire. A large Irish setter was sound asleep on the hearth. Clancy almost tripped, stepping on its tail as he sat down. It gave a little yelp. Without being asked, Liam came over with a pint of the usual and then retreated behind the bar.

Clancy slowly sipped his pint wondering what he had gotten himself into. It was supposed to be a quiet little holiday, a getaway from the office with no complications. He looked around. Doc Flannery was out on calls and the owner was in the back dealing with the trades people. A couple of middle-aged men who looked like farmers, in sweaters, jeans and boots were staring into the fire. They waved and mouthed cheers but made no effort to speak further.

Kathleen, the red headed, green eyed bar-maid a double for the late Maureen O'Hara, came over.

"A penny for your thoughts. You have been sitting here quiet as a mouse."

"Oh," said Clancy," just giving thought to what's been happing up at the Manor House. The Squire tripped on the stairs and now has a badly sprained ankle."

"Yes, so I heard. Well at least it's not broken."

"True," said Clancy.

"Well, if you need anything, let me know." Kathleen walked back to the bar.

The more he thought about it, his instincts as a cop were alerted. Something fishy was going but he couldn't put his finger on it. There had been too many accidents or near misses. First, there was the near car collision on their ride home from Blarney Castle. He would dismiss that one. It was probably some woman at the wheel who drove like a maniac. Next, there was the pigs escaping from their pen—someone had let them out. That could be anyone and maybe an accident. But it was no accident about the Squire's fall on the stairs.

All these incidents were somehow connected with the

squire. Was his life in danger? He suppressed that thought. He hadn't come over to Ireland to get mixed up in anything serious. He was on holiday and he wanted to enjoy himself, not to get involved and not to meddle in other people's affairs. It was probably all his imagination, even if he did see a pattern there.

After drinking his pint, he headed back to sit in the library with the Squire to keep him company before lunch.

Chapter 7

There was a heavy knock on the lounge door and a tall young man, with curly black hair, blue jeans and black leather jacket stuck his head in. He looks like a Murphy, thought Clancy.

"Uncle, I heard you had a nasty fall, so I came over to see how you are. How's the ankle?"

"Bad news travels fast. I have to keep off my feet, Quincy."

So, this was the young layabout the Squire had been talking about thought Clancy. He took a second look.

"When did it happen? How?" asked Quincy.

"Last night, in the middle of the night. I heard a noise. I thought someone was breaking in downstairs, so I went to investigate. I tripped and fell on the stairs. I twisted my ankle, but I don't think it's broken, thank heavens, but it's very painful. It's nice of you to come and see me. Haven't seen you for awhile. Help yourself to coffee and biscuits."

"Thanks, don't mind if I do." Quincy picked up a china mug and poured himself a cup of coffee out of the silver thermos. He looked at the plate displaying an array of biscuits and then picked a ginger one.

"What have you been up to, Quincy?"

"Nothing much. Helping out on the farm. I went into Cork to see what jobs they had to offer at the employment bureau. It's not for lack of trying. Nothing much."

"Well there'll be plenty of work around here, now that I have to keep off my feet. I'll hire you starting this morning."

"That's very good of you, uncle. I appreciate it."

"As soon as you finish your coffee, you can go and help your

43

brother. You will find him in the barn feeding the pigs and when that is finished, cleaning out the stalls."

"Will do. Thanks, uncle." He finished his coffee put the china mug down and left the room.

Young Quincy?" said Clancy nodding, in his direction. "Good of you to do that, Sean."

"Got to keep him occupied or he'll get into trouble."

A heavy tap on the door. Another visitor? Aren't we popular, thought Clancy. A large breasted, brassy blonde woman, in a blue cloak, thrust herself into the room. Now there's a woman I'd like an ankle massage from, thought Clancy. But she'd probably be too enthusiastic and overdo it.

The dog, got up from the hearth wagging its tail and sniffed at the woman's skirt.

"Down, kneel," said the Squire. The dog sat down obediently on the carpet beside the woman.

Taking in the room, she gave everyone a cheery smile. "I hope that I'm not disturbing you. Doc Flannery sent me over, Squire, to see if I can be of help. He can't come for the next couple of days, so he sent me. I'm the district nurse. My name is Tricia Busker and I brought along my assistant, Sabrina Mont."

A shy young woman, with long blond hair in braids and, blue eyes with a black Peabody jacket and jeans, had followed her into the room. Sabrina's quiet air was in sharp contrast to Tricia's upfront manner.

"Sabrina is a nurse in training and this is part of it I hope you won't mind having an extra person here?"

"We're delighted to have her company," replied the squire. "Don't stand on ceremony, do sit down."

Ms. Busker threw her cape into an empty chair, then strode over to the Squire, who was lying stretched out on the couch with his leg propped up on several pillows. "Here, let me have a look at your ankle." With a wide sweep, she threw the blanket on the floor and knelt beside him. "Got to unwind this bandage. Unroll it gently," she ordered Sabrina, Sabrina meekly did as she was told.

"Fine. Now, let's take a look."

What a huge bottom she has, thought Clancy glancing at the bent over figure, something to grab onto. I always liked big women.

"Doesn't look too bad." She paused, straightening up. "Doc Flannery said it wasn't broken. That it was just covered in black and purple bruises. I agree with him. It's coming along nicely. A bit yellow in some places but the swelling should go down soon. How is the pain? Do you need something for the pain?"

"Yes, it is very painful, said the Squire. "It's hard to sleep at night."

"Tylenol, extra strength with codeine, should do the trick. Now that I've seen it, we can wrap it up again. Stay off your feet. You won't be able to walk for a while." She dipped down, with those huge melon like breasts almost popping out of the top of her blouse, to wrap the ankle up again.

Clancy thought he would go blind, so much to see all in one go.

"Would you like a glass of sherry, Ms. Busker and Ms. Mont? It will keep the damp out. I'll send for Mansbridge," said the Squire.

"That's a nice idea." laughed Tricia, "I'll have to check on you more often. Who's your friend?" she said pointing to Clancy.

"My Canadian cousin, Clancy Murphy, he's come to visit me."

"How nice," she said, giving Clancy a long appraising look. "I hope you get around to seeing the sights. I have a little time off coming to me this week. Perhaps something can be arranged since the Squire can't get out and about. I'll be glad to take you around Cork. I've some Canadian cousins. I'd love to hear about Canada."

"That sounds nice and I look forward to it," said Clancy, thinking, while the cat's away the mice will play. Canada was far off in the distance, an ocean away when opportunity knocked.

After the ladies left, the Squire lay back on his pillow to get some rest. The housekeeper rang the bell. It was time for lunch, served buffet style. This time it was shepherd's pie and mushy peas. Mushy peas sounded vile, squashed green peas. They didn't serve that up in Mariposa.

After the meal was over, Clancy went upstairs and lay down for forty winks. Afterwards he went into the library. He told the Squire, who was resting his ankle, that he was going out to get some exercise and a breath of fresh air, down to The Crossroads.

The Squire thought it was great having Clancy in the house. He had been lonely since his wife died. Having hired help was not the same as your own flesh and blood. With no children, he was rumbling around this old house entirely on his own.

The Squire would have liked to have a drink with the locals, the neighbouring farmers. But he felt that his status wouldn't allow it. He was friendly when he met them on the road, in the village shops and in the spirits and wine shop, but still drew a line when it came to drinking with them.

It was his own fault that he was lonely. He was too sensitive, too much of an introvert. He blamed it on his upbringing, being brought up to remember he was a class apart. Foolishly, he clung to the old way of thinking.

***

The pub door was open. Inside, a fire was going in the grate. Liam Cross, was standing behind the bar. He greeted Clancy like a long-lost friend.

"I hear the Squire has twisted his ankle. What a shame. He's lucky to have you around to help. But what about your sightseeing? What will you do about that?"

"Tricia Busker, the nurse, has offered to help in that area."

"Not to worry. She's a fine lass and a fine nurse. You'll be in capable hands."

Yes, thought Clancy, very capable hands.

A big man, in muddy wellington boots, walked over to Clancy's table. He tipped his hat.

"I hear the Squire is laid up for awhile."

"News travels fast around here. You know him, do you?" Clancy looked at this big, middle-aged man, in dusty jeans and heavy knit sweater standing in from of him.

"I'm Jim Muir. I have a farm down the road from his. I bumped into Doc Flannery and he told me. He also told me that you were visiting from Canada.

"How are things going with him? He's a tight-fisted bastard. He's an ornery cuss. I've had some dealings with him in the past. He's as stubborn as a mule. Always wants to get his own way."

"Those are strong words," said Clancy.

"Telling it like it is. He's a tight wad. a real penny pincher. Never puts a twenty-cent piece, never mind a euro in the collection box after mass. Not him. He has no sympathy for the poor devils that don't have work and can't feed their wee ones. There's a lot of unemployment in these parts. My two sons can only get contract work in the city.

"But, as I was saying, my farm is down the road, next to his. He put up an electric fence around his pastures so that my cows can't drink from the nice little stream that flows alongside the edge of his property from mine. It's only a few metres away from my property. My cows need water and the mean bugger has put up a fence. We have to truck in water, which can be expensive. There was

46

a big protest here about the water rates not long ago. This fence wasn't there in the old days. His father looked the other way. We were good neighbours then. There have been changes with him and they haven't been good. He never makes a courtesy call over to my house on the holidays. I used to sip a glass of sherry to welcome in the New Year with the old Squire, but not with him."

"That's too bad," said Clancy. "I'm just visiting in these parts. On holidays."

"You are, are you? Well I'm going to have a pint and then get back to work. There is always something to do there. See you around."

Clancy sat there nursing his drink and staring into the fire. "There's one suspect," he thought. Just then the door flew opened and in walked Tricia and Sabrina.

"Won't you come over here and join me?" he asked.

Tricia flashed him a big smile. "We've spent this morning and afternoon making the rounds and have developed a big appetite for a late lunch."

Tricia slipped into a place beside Clancy leaving Sabrina to take a chair opposite them.

Squeezed in by two attractive Irish Colleens. "How nice," thought Clancy.

Tricia put her hand on his. "I have some spare time tomorrow morning, I could take you into Cork to see the sights while I do a few errands and then take you back to the manor in time for tea, or whatever. Are you game?"

"That sounds nice. With the Squire laid up and not being able to get about, I would not get much opportunity to get around and sight see. This sounds like a nice idea. I'd would be very open to joining you. Will Sabrina come too?"

Sabrina lowered her eyes and blushed, saying that she was otherwise engaged. Clancy noted the blush.

"Then it's settled. Tomorrow morning," said Tricia.

Chapter 8

Promptly at 9 a.m., Tricia was in the driveway, waiting for him in her black Volkswagen. "Hop in." She leaned over and opened the door. He squeezed in beside her. She leaned against him, as she opened the glove compartment, her knockers pressing against him. Cozy, thought Clancy. She fiddled in the compartment until she found a map. "This is our route into Cork. Off we go."

Tricia drove fast around the curves in the road, so fast that Clancy was thrown against her several times and had to apologize as he made contact. Was this deliberate on her part? But maybe that was the whole idea. He feared that sooner or later they would end up in a ditch. He expected her, being a nurse and all, to be a slow, careful driver. But he was clearly mistaken. It also made him think that she was the woman driver who had almost put the Squire and himself off the road on their way back from Blarney Castle.

It was a lovely fall day, the beech and sycamore tree leaves that lined the road had turned the colour of yellow, russet and brown.

On the way into Cork, they drove over several bridges "Cork, Ireland's second largest city was built over two rivers," remarked Tricia as she dropped him off in the city centre.

"There's lots to see around the centre, particularly if you want to sit down and rest your feet. Walk around the centre of the city, taking in St. Fin Barres, a lovely gothic cathedral."

"Did you know there's also a statue to Father Theobald Matthew, who was a staunch tea drinker and advocate for abstinence from liquor. He was one of the founders of the Cork Total Abstinence Society in 1838. In his time, he was not a popular fellow. Like everyone else, the Irish are fond of their drink. But they must have changed their minds as they erected a statue in his honour. It's up on St. Patrick Street, if you care to find it. Being a police officer, you also might want to look in at the Old Gaol, now a museum."

"Nah, I'm on vacation. I've got enough of that stuff at home. I'll wander around by myself taking in the sights."

"Anyway, there's lots to look at. I'm busy until 11a.m, then we can meet at Starbucks."

Passing another coffeehouse, a couple on the periphery of the patio caught his attention. It looked liked Quincy Murphy, Hugh's boy, sitting with Sabrina Mont. So that was what her appointment was all about. He looked away, he didn't want them to see him and think that he was snooping.

A swoop of young girls, with mini skirts flapping in the breeze, passed him laughing.

"Oh, to be young again," thought Clancy. "I think I'll just stand on the bridge and look at the quay, the boats, the warehouses, the restaurants and pubs and smell the ocean breezes." In the distance he could see sandy beaches and rugged cliffs. While, below, the ocean waves broke against the rocks and the sand. Seabirds—gannets and razor bills soared over the blue waters. A large gannet did a vertical dive into the wave, coming up with a fish in its bill.

Time passed quickly

Worried a little that he might get lost, he retraced his footsteps, to the corner, where he remembered the names of certain shops.

He was soon back at Starbucks where Tricia was waiting for him at a table. "Enjoy the sights?" she asked.

"Yes, there's lots to see. Can't take it all in, though in one day." He was on the point of mentioning that he had seen Quincy and Sabrina, but he didn't think it was a good idea. It was Sabrina's business not his.

"It has been a great morning. I've really appreciated your kindness to me."

"No problem. We'll have to get together again before you leave. Maybe meet in the pub some evening." Under the table, he felt her foot vigorously rubbing his. She's playing footsie with me. If she doesn't stop soon, she will wear out the leather on my shoe. I wonder how long I can keep her at bay. After all, I am a married man. But who is to know if something were to happen between the two of us? We are both consenting adults and it might be my only chance to have a fling. Who would know? There are no witnesses. Clancy felt that he had a lot of serious thinking to do.

"That's a good idea. My vacation so far has been most enjoyable." said Clancy nudging her knee under the table. "Well, it's time to head back to the Manor House. I told the Squire I would be back in time for lunch."

Getting out of the car, he gave her a brief kiss, but Tricia suddenly grabbed him and gave him a real smacker on the lips. "Wow! What a hottie!" thought Clancy.

Chapter 9

Lunch hadn't been served yet, so Clancy wandered into the library, went over to the bookshelves and took down once again, the book on the Murphy genealogy. Then he found a nice, fat. leather chair to sit in by the fire. He flipped the pages back to the 1800s. During the great famine, one of his relatives, an indentured farm hand, had a family of ten children who were starving. So, one afternoon he stole a sheep which had wandered too close to his land from the neighbouring farm. He thought the Squire wouldn't miss the lamb he took, forgetting that all the sheep were counted at the end of the day. He was hunted down. The county court presided over by an English judge, ruled for capital punishment. He was hanged, leaving behind a wife and ten children to starve in the famine of that year. Fortunately, some of the descendants survived and are alive today.

Mansbridge interrupted his reading. He announced. "Á visitor to see you," and rolled his eyes heavenward. "Sister Gertrude."

A stout woman, about medium height in a grey suit, and white blouse, with a big silver cross hanging from her neck, strode into the room. Her hair was cropped short and, on her feet, she had the ugliest looking shoes, black Oxfords, that Clancy had ever seen on a woman. Rather butch, thought Clancy. Fat ankles, thick neck, close cropped hair, large hands and big feet made her appear more like a man than a woman. She was not feminine at all.

He recognized her type right away, as a take charge battle axe. There was no doubt about it. He had come across them before.

One drop kick from her and you could be permanently crippled.

"Hello everyone. Let me introduce myself. I'm Sister Gertrude and have been assigned to this parish."

"What brings you here?" inquired the Squire, as politely as he could. "Do take a seat. Mansbridge will get you a glass of sherry."

Sister Gertrude plumped herself down heavily in a nearby chair with a sigh, pulling down her skirts to cover her knobby knees.

"I haven't seen you at mass, Squire Murphy, for several weeks. I heard from other church-goers that you've sprained your ankle. So, I came over to offer you a prayer and a blessing. I have a small silver medal of Saint Christopher that I want to give you."

"Very thoughtful," said the Squire, taking a hard look at her. "Very thoughtful, but I think I'll take a rain cheque on the prayer and the blessing.

"But prayer is good for the soul," remonstrated Sister Gertrude, fingering her cross. "If all else fails, try prayer. Prayer might speed up your recovery."

Clancy thought, "What a dicey situation. If he continues to refuse, is Sister Gertrude going to send down a thunderbolt from heaven and strike us all dead?"

"If you insist, I will accept the St. Christopher medal."

Out of her big, black leather purse. She took a small cloth bag, lifted it up to the light and extracted a small silver medal. She kissed it, before handing it over to him. "There," she said proudly." May God bless you and keep you."

"Very kind, very kind," murmured the Squire, fingering the medal, looking at it from side to side. "How do you like your sherry, sweet or dry?"

"Sweet," said Sister Gertrude. "I see you have a visitor staying with you. A relation?"

"Yes, "said Clancy. "I'm a very distant cousin."

"Well, I hope you get to see a bit of Ireland while you're here. That's an American accent?"

"No, I'm Canadian."

"So sorry, no offense. Well I must be off. Time never waits for the wicked," she chuckled, "and the wicked are all around us." She glanced around the room, then out the door she went.

"Thank heavens she's gone," said the Squire, breathing a sigh of relief. "What a pain in the butt."

***

Clancy was telling the Squire how his trip had gone into Cork and what a beautiful city it was and how grateful he was to Tricia for the ride there, when there was another knock at the library door.

"Who could it be this time?" asked the Squire.

"I have a Mr. Hunter, a local amateur archeologist, at the front door. He urgently wishes to speak to you."

"Show him in. Although I've never met him before, it'll be interesting to hear what he has to say," said the Squire.

A tall man, wearing a cloth cap, jacket and jeans, came into the room in his stockinged feet. Around his neck hung a pair of binoculars. "Excuse my stockinged feet, the boots are too muddy for such a grand place as this." He put down his walking stick and backpack in a nearby chair. "Thank you for giving me an audience. Let me introduce myself. I'm a visiting archeologist from Trinity College, Dublin. I specialize in the classical period, Greek and Roman ruins. I spend my weekends hiking in the countryside, partly for exercise and partly for what artifacts I might discover. I was driving by on my way home and decided to pop in and tell you about my latest find. I think you might be interested."

"Offer him a glass of sherry, Mansbridge. Don't keep standing. Do take a seat."

Mansbridge poured out a glass and handed it to Mr. Hunter.

"Today I was alone, hiking on the adjourning farm, Jim Muir's farm, and I went into the woodlot which joins your property. I did it out of curiosity. I was able to get over the stile into your property and came to an open area. This, I believe, was where that unfortunate accident happened with your brother's boy I'd read about it in the papers.

"There was a stream and I decided to wander along it, on a whim, no apparent reason. Then, I found something interesting. Often discoveries arise out of serendipity. It took my breath away. I'd chanced upon a huge granite boulder lying next to the stream. It was a large wide rectangular slab, about two metres in height, standing on its own. I thought, this looks interesting and, as I examined it further, with its indentations where the cups, bowls, and candles for the mass could stand, I came to the conclusion that it might be another Mass Rock. There are quite a few of them found in the County Cork countryside some on private farm land, others in woods. This could be one. People would come and celebrate mass in the evening or when they thought the authorities were not about during the Penal Period, under Cromwell. If they had practiced saying mass during that period and were caught, they would have been executed by the English army."

"Interesting observation," said the Squire, nodding. "Do continue."

Clancy took another sip of coffee. He grimaced. It was only luke warm. He would have to ask Mansbridge to top it up. He'd much prefer a pint down the road. He was not much use to anyone at this point. As a guest he could just listen, be a fly on the wall, which was all that was required of him. History about a large rock didn't turn him on that much.

"This is pure speculation, but the rock was in a large clearing which had room for a possible one hundred worshipers. An archeological survey will have to be conducted so that we might know for sure. We're going back centuries."

"If it proves to be a Mass Rock, do you think that in the future, you that you might set some of the land aside, a small portion for visitors? People will give the land surrounding a Mass Rock a name. It will be thought of as a sacred place."

"Oh, really. I never thought of that. I will give it some thought. But then, we don't know for sure if this is a Mass Rock."

"I'll go into the woodlot again at a later time in the week and have a second look. I'm just an academic and I do this just as a hobby. I'm not a government expert. Do I have your permission?"

"Most certainly, I wouldn't want to impede any investigation into the heritage of Cork County. But I'm not keen on taking down the fence. It was expensive to put in. I don't want the neighbourhood to be tramping through my land. It reduces the value of the property, of the land, if I ever want to sell some of it."

"I understand your concerns. In the meantime, with your permission, I'll notify the archeological society and see if they want to do a survey to authenticate the rock. Thanks for your kind remarks and for the sherry." He then picked up his backpack and Mansbridge let him out.

After he left, Clancy got up and went into the Great Hall. He wanted to find out what was going on at the office with another call to Greg. The last call hadn't been very satisfying, because the connection was poor. The line was busy. He wondered what was going on in Mariposa.

***

One patient after another had trooped into Dr. Sandy's waiting room. It seemed to him that it was like an assembly line at the canning factory. He paused and took a long, lingering look outside at the street. The sun was still shining, beckoning him to come out. It was a gorgeous fall day. How he would love to drop everything and stretch his legs, go for a walk and end up with a quick coffee at Apple Annie's. He paused for a moment to think over the cases that he had seen in the last little while. Half his patients had come in with hemorrhoids and constipation complaints. Eat more roughage, more fruit and vegetables," he told them. "Drink more water, drink a glass of water at night and first thing in the morning." He had seen several cases of shingles, the itch that never ends and keeps reoccurring in middle-aged patients. But when he advised them to get a shingles shot, not paid for by OHIP, they refused because of the cost.

But of all his cases, the hardest diagnosis was for cancer of the ovaries. His women patients would dismiss bloating, gas and pain as menopausal symptoms and would put off seeing him. That was the case this morning. The middle-aged Mrs. X had put off seeing him and just dismissed her symptoms as 'change of life' symptoms

He had requested an ultrasound. Thankfully he had caught it in time. So many cases that he had heard of were too late and the women had progressed to stage four cancer. It was known as the hidden killer of women, but it could be cured, if caught in time.

He took off his glasses and wiped them. The other thing to watch out for was when coughs never went away, no matter how you treated them. This could be an indication of something more serious. a precursor of cancer of the lung, or leukemia.

He needed a break, to smell fresh air and to stretch his legs, but his patients were waiting. He sighed.

Interrupting his reverie was the voice of Miss Hornby. "Your next patient, Miss Temple. Should I send her in?" said Miss Hornby, poking her head around the door.

"Yes, of course." He knew Miss Temple, a wiry old biddy who never had anything wrong with her. She had good genes. Both of her parents had lived into their nineties. After a few minutes he went into the examining room.

"I'm here for a check up. My heart has been fluttering," said Miss Temple, pressing her hand to her breast.

He appraised her body, this scrawny chicken, this flat chested old lady with wisps of white hair, wearing a shapeless blue skirt.

She came every three months to have a check up and have

him listen to her heart. What an eccentric old lady. He wrapped the cuff around her skinny arm to take her blood pressure. One twenty over seventy-two. He was disappointed to see that it was normal. Next, he bent over the old lady's heart with his stethoscope. She smelled of talcum powder and cod liver oil.

"Your heart is ticking over nicely," he said, straightening up and looking her squarely in the eye. Impulsively he pinched her on the cheek. "You're going to outlive us all, Miss Temple. You will live to be a hundred. You have an iron constitution. It must be the wee dram of whisky that you take every night before you go to bed."

He gave her a slight tap on her bony knee to see if her reflexes were working. They were. The skinny old ladies, he thought, lasted much longer than the fat ones with their high blood pressure, high cholesterol and diabetes.

"I hope not, I'm getting a bit arthritic in the knees and joints. My heart starts to flutter occasionally. As for drinking, liquor never touched my lips."

Doctors do take liberties, the young ones are worse than the older ones, thought Miss Temple, All this pinching on the cheek and pats on the head. She was no child.

"What a shame," said Dr. Sandy, knowing how much he enjoyed his glass of sherry at the end of the working day. "It's good for the arteries, keeps the blood flowing nicely. Well, nothing appears unusual that I can lay a finger on." He pinched her cheek again, laughing at his little joke.

"Humph," thought Miss Temple quickly buttoning up her white blouse. "Oh my," she suddenly exclaimed, "my mother's brooch, I just took it off. I laid it down and now it's gone. I can't lose that. It's a family heirloom. My dead mother would be horrified."

"Hold on, I'll take a look around," said Dr. Sandy.

He got down on his hands and knees to humour her. It wasn't the first time that an old lady had mislaid some valuable items in the examining room. The last time, a patient with dementia had lost her change purse and there was a great to do about that.

Miss Temple wailed. "It was a cameo, a lovely blue cameo pin which she gave me a few years before dying, with a sterling silver clasp. Oh my, what am I going to do? It's very valuable."

"Is it?" asked Dr. Sandy. It was not the first time an old lady had lost a valuable piece of jewellery which was later discovered to have been bought at Dollarama or the Salvation Army Thrift Shop.

"You say you had it on you when you came into the examining room. You changed here before I came in. Are you sure that you wore it here and it isn't still at home on your bedside table? I'll have my nurse look around in the waiting room. It may have fallen off there."

He opened the door, "Miss Hornby will you have a quick look around the waiting room? Miss Temple seems to have lost her cameo brooch."

"Yes, doctor." Miss Hornby got up from her desk and walked over to the chairs and looked under them. A woman got out of her way, so she could poke in the corner. Then she looked at the table where the magazines were stacked. "Can't see anything so far. We'll will contact you, Miss Temple if it shows up. I have your phone number."

Miss Temple made a flustered exit from the doctor's office. Am I losing my mind? she wondered. I'm sure that I was wearing it when I left home. On the way home, she decided to drop into the police station, just in case someone had found it in the street and turned it in. She would need to contact the police anyway, for insurance purposes.

It was just a short walk down Mississauga. She opened the door. The duty sergeant, recognizing her on sight, groaned when he saw her approach. This was not the first, nor would it be the last time he had had to deal with Miss Temple. Patience, he told himself. She is a tax-payer and a member of the general public. Be gentle.

"I'm here to report the theft of my brooch. It was either stolen or lost at the doctor's office. I just came from there and they can't find it."

"Oh, really, and what kind of a brooch was that, the kind you find in a cracker jack box? Just kidding."

How rude. "It's an antique brooch left to me by my mother. A cameo. Very valuable."

"In that case I'll write up a report. Theft under $1,000. It'll just take me a minute."

"Don't hurry. I've got all the time in the world."

"I'm sure you have. But I haven't. Sign here and put the date. I'll give you a copy for insurance purposes. The insurance policies usually have a $200.00 deductible. So, I think that your brooch might not be worth that much, eh? After the deductible is taken off."

"It is valuable," huffed Miss Temple and snatched the form from him.

After the police station, she thought, I'll go home and look for it again. Then I will pick up a paper to read up on the obituaries. Mrs. Reed has pneumonia and she's sure to pass on soon. Mrs.

Thincrisp has laryngitis, a terrible cough and chest pains. She, I predict, will soon be pushing up daisies. I hate to see them go. It gets lonely being old with all your friends dying off. But the funerals make up for it. They're a nice outing. At the receptions afterwards, there are sandwiches, nice cakes and pastries, although, I sometimes get tired of eating egg salad and tuna fish. I prefer roast beef. I can slip a few into the plastic bag that I keep handy in my purse. I'd won't need to eat supper afterwards.

***

After half an hour Clancy tried the line again, "Is that you? The line's a bit scratchy. You sound as if you have a cold."

"No, it's the line. I have too much on my plate. I'm all stressed out. Yesterday, a young girl called Claire came to the office to show me her pet rabbit that she'd taken to the fall fair to meet the judges. Shoo, shoo I told her, get lost. You know what rabbits do. I'm tired of cleaning up.

"Dogs are biting the mailmen, old ladies want to piss in our toilet, and instead go on the floor. It's an emergency they tell me. I'm tired of mopping up. Your little friend keeps asking for you, they haven't found her brooch. She needs papers for the insurance company. I give them to her, but she keeps losing them and comes back to the office for a copy. Keeps pestering me. You've been too friendly to her, too kind. I'm on the verge of a nervous breakdown. I want to concentrate on my break-and-enter cases, but all these little old ladies are driving me nuts."

"When you see the old lady who wants to use the toilet coming, lock the doors."

"I tried that. But then she pounded away at the front door and started screaming. She caused an awful ruckus the last time. Police harassment, someone beating her up is what the pedestrians on the street thought. I had to let her in to shut her up."

"Simply say, the toilet is busted. Establish perimeters between yourself and the public. No one can go beyond a certain point. Lay down on the floor a yellow line right in front of the counter. I expect that yellow tape to be down on the floor in front of the counter by the time I get back. Stop being a pussy. Put some steel in your shorts. Put some lead in your pencil. Stop shooting blanks."

"Put some what? What? Shooting blanks?"

"Put some, oh forget it. I'll call back again when the line is better." He rang off.

Chapter 10

Clancy and the Squire were having afternoon tea and ginger biscuits in the library. Clancy took a biscuit and dipped into his hot coffee. The Squire looked away pretending not to notice. Instead, he reached down beside the sofa for a cushion and placed it under his ankle saying. "That feels more comfortable." Dipping your biscuit, realized Clancy, was not a classy thing to do in front of the Squire.

There was a knock at the door. "Sister Gertrude," announced Mansbridge, stepping into the room. rolling his eyes.

Sister Gertrude, red in the face, was breathing heavily. "I'm so excited, I could just burst from happiness. I was slipping into the pub, The Crossroads, I don't go there to do much drinking, I just use the occasion to collect money to repair our parish church roof. It leaks, it needs repairing. Serendipity happened. I met a visiting archeologist from Dublin, Mr. Hunter, who informed me that there might be a Mass Rock in your woodlot. This is wonderful news. A Mass Rock by the stream, in your woodlot, where masses used to take place in ancient times when Catholics in the countryside were persecuted for saying mass. This makes it a sacred space, *Carraig an aitrinn.* I rushed right over to see what you might know about it."

"We don't know for sure," murmured the Squire not too happily. "I don't want people to get too excited about it until some professional archeologists have a good look at it and confirm that it is. It's only a rumour at this point. Mr. Hunter is an academic, not a field archeologist. He found it and thinks it has the potential to be that."

"I certainly hope it's a Mass Rock. It would do so much for the community and for our faith," sighed Sister Gertrude, clasping her hands to her bosom. "We could have annual masses said there in the summer, and then special services in the winter. It could become a pilgrimage to a sacred space. Who knows? The possibilities are endless. Maybe someone would have a vision of the Virgin Mary near the rock, like Our Lady of Guadeloupe in Mexico City. Think of all the things that might happen. Word would spread throughout Ireland. Tourists would come from all over, even from Canada and America. All kinds of good things might happen."

Clancy, who was sitting there listening quietly, thought, the poor old dear was really getting worked up about a bit of rock. Probably nothing will come of the findings. Not much must be happening in the countryside if they get into a flap about this, a large rock. There must be thousands of them.

"I must go and see if I can find it. It shouldn't be too difficult, knowing the size of it and that it's in the woodlot, close to the stream on your property. That's a good enough description for me," said Sister Gertrude.

"Be careful. It's muddy out there and the hunting season begins today. Are you sure that this is a good idea? You shouldn't go alone. Take someone with you. You might trip on a stone or log and twist your ankle and no one would know you were there," warned the Squire.

"Nonsense. I'm perfectly safe. It's a sacred space where the rock sits. I must be off while the light is still good."

Sister Gertrude confidently strode out of the room. They heard the door slam. Clancy could picture her, her arms swinging, striding along the road like a sergeant major towards the woodlot. She was on a mission to find a sacred rock.

***

Clancy went up to his bedroom and took off his shoes and put his feet up for a quick cat nap. When he woke up he decided to stretch his legs and get some fresh air. He let himself out the side door, walking past the driveway. He noticed that Sister Gertrude's little black Austin was still parked there. That's odd. It's been over two hours since she'd been in to visit them. Surely, she would have found the rock by now. He got a funny feeling, call it a copper's gut instinct. He went inside and located Mansbridge.

In a casual voice he asked, "Have you seen Sister Gertrude around? Her car is still in the driveway."

"No, not since she sailed out of here several hours ago to find the rock."

"I think I'll go and have a wander down there and check to see if everything's alright. One can easily twist one's ankle in the undergrowth by the woods and stream and not be able to walk because of the pain."

"Oh, she'll be back soon," said Mansbridge confidently. "Don't worry about her. She will survive. When the ship goes down, Sister Gertrude will be on the life raft." He laughed at his little joke.

"Nah, walking down there will give me a good excuse to work up an appetite before dinner."

Clancy sauntered down the dirt road towards the woodlot. Leaving the dirt road, he ducked his head under some branches and followed the beaten path of fallen leaves and sand, noticing the large mushrooms clustered at the base of a tree. Don't pick, he told himself, edible or poisonous, he couldn't tell. The grass and leaves were wet and slippery. Next time he'd borrow a walking stick. Ahead of him he could hear the gurgle of a stream.

He looked around to get his bearings. There was no sign of Sister Gertrude, not even her footprints in the soil. He looked at where the branches had broken to assure himself that he was on the right path. He listened for the sound of movement in the bush, but there was none, just utter stillness. He thought he might see a fox or a rabbit shoot by but there was no sudden movement. Then ahead, he saw several, large, black crows circling overhead an ominous sign

"Maybe she's gone back another way and I've missed her altogether," he thought.

Ah, here's the stream, now to follow it. The rock must be close by.

His leather boots sank into the muddy ground. There were small boulders strewn around the edges of the stream making his path slippery. Ahead, he saw a massive, grey boulder. He listened again for a voice or some movement, but he heard nothing. There was no sign of Sister Gertrude. He felt a strong premonition that things weren't going to turn out well. Just call it a copper's instinct.

This massive grey granite slab ahead must be the rock they were talking about.

He slowly walked to the end of the slab and looked along the shelf to the other end. Then he noticed red splashes on the stone. Blood? He bent down to see where it was coming from. He smelled the sweet, sticky smell of death. He knew without looking that there was a body lying in the leaves next to the stone. Bending over he

65

recognized it as the massive body of Sister Gertrude, lying in a heap, her legs splayed out, her grey skirt gathered up around her knees, her cloak spread over the ground with part of her skull, the front of her head, blown off. Her dull eyes stared up at him. Clumps of blood and brain matter were scattered on the ground. He didn't touch her or attempt to roll her over, but stood back taking it all in. It was a shocking sight.

Poor Sister Gertrude had come to a nasty end. Did a hunter shoot her mistaking her for an animal? It had happened not too recently, he thought. The blood had dried on the stone, probably a couple of hours ago.

He pulled out his cell phone to call the Gardai. "A woman has been killed in the woodlot on Squire Murphy's farm."

"Who are you?"

"I'm Clancy Murphy, a visiting relation, who discovered the body. I'll wait until you get here. Here are the directions."

A good twenty minutes went by and then a car drove up followed by another car and a van with the label on its side in large letters, 'Forensics.' Clancy stood on the edge of the woodlot waiting for them. "Over here." He led them down to the creek and along its bank to the stone where the body lay.

"Have you touched anything?" asked a blond-haired Colleen, taking out her notepad.

"No," and he flashed his Canadian ID. "I'm on vacation. I didn't set out to find a body. That was the least thing I expected to find."

"Do you recognize the body?"

"I recognize the body as that of Sister Gertrude. She dropped into the Manor House about three hours ago and then left to find a large Mass Rock, or so she claimed. I thought something was wrong when she didn't return after a couple of hours and collect her car. I set out to find her. I thought she'd twisted her ankle or something, not this."

"When did you find the body?"

"About fifteen minutes ago. I phoned you right away."

The two fresh faced police constables from the first car looked rather young, but he figured they must be competent or they wouldn't have that job. He left them to do their work. Don't meddle, they won't appreciate it, he told himself, you're on vacation. He informed them that he was staying at the Squire's manor if they needed to ask him further questions. One of them said they would be in touch with him.

He walked back up the dirt road to the Manor House to tell the sad news to the Squire. Sister Gertrude had come to a violent end. Half her head had been blown off. She'd been shot with a rifle, probably by a hunter.

"What?' said the Squire on hearing the news. "I can't believe it. Alive one minute and then dead the next. I saw police cars go down the road, but it never crossed my mind that someone had been murdered."

He shook his head. "Unlucky woman. Maybe some hunters mistook her for an animal. We warn people not to go wandering in the woods at this time of year. If they do, we tell them to wear bright coloured clothing. The colour grey that she was wearing blended in with the landscape. I like to think it was a hunter who made a mistake, not someone intending to deliberately kill her." He sighed. "But she insisted on going down there and there was no way we could stop her. Once she got the idea of finding the Mass Rock that was all she could think of.

"It's too bad that it happened in that location. That's become an unlucky spot, two deaths now have happened there. It makes you wonder. What do you think, Clancy? Is it a bad omen? Is there a curse on the woodlot?"

"I am not superstitious. I don't believe in omens." said Clancy, deep in thought. "Too many things have happened, your fall on the stair, and now this that can't be easily explained away," he mused.

He shook his head, "Why anyone would kill a harmless old lady is beyond me. It wasn't for money or for sex. Too old for sex and she had no money. She was religious. What could possibly be the motive? I'd never heard of a Sister being murdered in Canada.

Clancy rang Father Flynn. "I have bad news for you. It's difficult to tell you this. Sister Gertrude was killed in the woodlot possibly shot by mistake by a hunter."

"Oh, how awful. This is appalling news. When did it happen?"

"Several hours ago."

"I'll have to contact the mother house in Dublin. The Reverend Mother will contact members of her family. I think her parents are dead. She had one brother who's a priest in America. He has to be notified.

"Funeral arrangements must be made. We could have a mass said here in this parish then have the hearse take the body to Dublin. The sisters will want a funeral mass at the Mother House followed by a Christian burial in Holy Cross cemetery."

"Let us know if there is anything we can do to help," said Clancy.

The Squire, who had been listening in to the conversation, turned to Clancy.

"I know that you're on vacation, at leisure so to speak, but this accident has happened in the same place as the accident with Seamus and we need your skill set. It leaves me bewildered as to how anyone could make such a mistake in my woodlot. It would be a great favour to me, Clancy, if you would put on your policeman's hat and investigate this, or at least lend a hand."

"No, no, I don't believe in butting into your affairs. I'm a guest in another country I have no authority here, no credentials. The Gardai might not like it. The local police don't want a stranger to tread on their territory. They might think I was destroying evidence or manipulating things. They would be highly suspicious of my efforts."

"But it wouldn't be butting in," protested the Squire. "You could just poke around on your own, quietly asking questions. That wouldn't be too difficult. I am asking you as a personal favour to me."

"Well, I can poke around if you want. There's no harm in that. If I do it discreetly and not get anyone's hackles up."

"Good, then that's settled. That's a load off my shoulders."

"What it means is getting the names of everyone in the pub that was there this afternoon and interviewing them. What I will do, is ask them who they were talking to. Their memories might not be reliable, especially after a few drinks."

"Doc Flannery might be able to help and Mr. Muir and my brother, they're usually in the pub. I'd appreciate any help you can give us."

"Don't count on anything much," said Clancy, "but I will do what I can."

***

It was getting late and both Clancy and the Squire had decided to retire for the night when a knock came at the library door. Mansbridge entered and announced, "Father Flynn".

Father Flynn entered the room dressed in his black suit and white clerical collar, He appeared to be in his early forties, a slender man, with an open face. He could be considered handsome, with his thick, black curly hair and rosy cheeks, the picture of good health. "In another life," Clancy thought, "he would have been a successful farmer."

Mansbridge reached for the sherry decanter, poured a glass and handed it wordlessly to Father Flynn who made the sign of the cross.

"I shouldn't be calling on you this late, but I nipped in on the chance that you would be here laid up with your ankle. I'm sorry to hear what happened. After you phoned, the Gardai notified me about Sister Gertrude. Dreadful. The body won't be released for several days until after the autopsy. Then, we can make arrangements.

"I've just come from blessing the sick, a young woman in a semi-coma. I made the sign of the cross over her heart. In doing so, I accidentally touched her breast. She'd been in a semi-coma for days after a car accident in when she'd been thrown through the windshield. Immediately, she sat up and opened her eyes and looked straight at me. Her mother, who'd been sitting in a chair by the bed for days on end, exclaimed "This is a miracle. We've not much hope for our daughter. Our prayers have been answered, Isn't that wonderful?" asked Father Flynn.

"I've come to do an exorcism, at the Mass Rock to purge ourselves of the evil that lingers there. I feel it's important if we are going to get beyond this tragedy. To put closure on what happened. I'll be very glad to do it."

"That's very thoughtful of you," said the Squire. "Sister Gertrude was an enthusiast, a woman on a mission."

"Such a dreadful end. She was active, cut down in her prime when she was most helpful," nodded Father Flynn.

"No, no exorcism needed," shuddered the Squire. "Imagine all those people tramping around, knocking over fences, leaving gates open, letting the animals loose. No, I'd prefer not to have it. "Instead, I'll give you a generous donation to say a mass for the soul of Sister Gertrude.

"Mansbridge, will you get my cheque book out of my desk? Have you found it? Good." He wrote a figure on it and handed the cheque to Father Flynn.

"Most generous, most generous," murmured Father Flynn lightly kissing the cheque, then quickly slipping it into his vest pocket.

"I only met her briefly. What was she like?" asked Clancy wondering who would want to kill this harmless old bird.

"She was very involved in parish work, separating she said, the wheat from the chaff. She took a tough stance against those who didn't not follow the church's rules. Sister Gertrude was very, how shall I say, rigid in pursuit of the rules of the church. Especially divorced Catholics who were not allowed to receive the host during mass. She was not liberal in the spirit of Pope Francis. I pleaded ignorance. If I barred divorced Catholics from the services, I would soon have an empty church."

"Oh, said Clancy, intrigued, "and who might they be, these divorced Catholics?"

"I can give you an example. Your neighbor, Farmer Muir. Since his wife ran off with another man, he's had another woman from the village move in with him. They're living together as man and wife, so it seems, in Sister Gertrude's eyes, that was a sin."

"So, Sister Gertrude's restriction on their receiving the host was pointless, as they don't even come to mass. But before that, when they bumped into Sister Gertrude in the pub, she made her feelings known.

"Oh dear, my glass is almost empty," said Father Flynn, looking absentmindedly down at his glass.

"Another one, Father?" asked Mansbridge, presenting the crystal decanter.

"'Don't mind if I do. "He knocked it back with gusto. "This will keep the chill off. It's been wonderful to talk to you about my concerns and I will say a mass for the soul of Sister Gertrude. In the meantime, I have to go and visit the sick and those who need my counsel. I won't neglect you, Squire, and I'll visit again." He made his way out.

"Pleasant fellow," said Clancy.

"Yes," replied the Squire, "when he's sober."

***

"Phone call for you, Sir. Do you want to take it in here?" asked Mansbridge

"Here would be fine."

Mansbridge handed him the phone, whispering, "It's the Gardai."

"Clancy Murphy here."

"This is Sergeant Finney investigating the murder of Sister

70

Gertrude. Mr. Murphy. You are our only witness. We're having difficulty in finding any witnesses. Did you see anyone when you were walking towards the woodlot? Did you pass anyone coming away? Anyone in the woodlot? Anyone at all in the vicinity? Try and remember."

"To all those questions, I answer an unqualified no. I saw no one at all. I walked along the road alone, there and back. How far away do you figure the killer was when she was shot?"

"We believe the killer was within several metres of her, according to the wound that she experienced. It's possible the gunman was behind trees and didn't see her and shot her accidentally. However, there's a large open space in front of the rock and not much foliage to obstruct one's view, so we think whoever shot her, knew her and recognized her. We think she was shot in the head as she was trying to get away. We don't think it was an accident and we can't blame it on a hunter. We'll be continuing our investigation in the area and search the ground for bullet casings."

"So, you don't think it was a hunter out looking for foxes and wolves and that it was an accident? You think it was someone she knew?"

"We don't know for sure. How many people knew that she was going exploring? That's the question. She went alone to the woodlot. She told you and the Squire."

"Well here I am, and the Squire is laid up with a twisted ankle. She was in the pub at the end of the road before coming to our place. That's where she heard about the Mass Rock from Mr. Hunter, the archeologist. She told everyone that she wanted to see it."

"If so, did she tell the people at the pub where she was going? This would widen the number of suspects considerably. Thanks for your help." Sergeant Finney rang off.

Chapter 11

The autopsy for Sister Gertrude was scheduled for several days later. She had been shot once in the back of the head. Half her head had been blown off. Sergeant Finney asked Clancy if he would like to come and hear the details. Clancy knew it wouldn't be pretty and went reluctantly.

The autopsy was to be held in a Cork hospital. Sergeant Finney would pick him up and drive him there.

"We need your input, Clancy, as you were one of the last people to see her alive."

It was a small hospital on the outskirts of Cork, a limestone building built around the turn of the century, but with a modern glass front entrance. They went in and headed for the basement.

"You're just on time." said Dr. O' Malley wearing a pair of goggles and gown. He waved his gloved hand in greeting. "Go into the next room and put on don the appropriate gear, so we don't leave behind any trace material or get infected by micro organisms."

It took Clancy a few minutes to don the suit, put on shoe covers, protective gloves and a face mask.

A technician wheeled the gurney carrying the body of Sister Gertrude out from the freezer. Dr. O'Malley checked the name tag tied to the toe and nodded.

"Here we have a 52-year-old female who has sustained a bullet wound to the back of the head."

Clancy stared down at this dead middle-aged woman, lying naked before him, hardly believing that she had once been a nun shielded from men's eyes. She would never have allowed her body to be exposed as such. Death held no dignity for Sister Gertrude.

What remained of her head flopped to one side on the steel block that held it.

Dr. O'Malley went over her body with a magnifying glass and tweezers. In his spare hand he held a tape recorder. "No sign of bruising, scratches, or defense wounds on her arms. No skin under the fingernails. She didn't fight off the attacker. The attacker must have caught her by surprise, or else was known to her.

"She was a virgin. There was no penetration or sexual interference or bruising on the thighs or vaginal areas."

"Aren't all nuns virgins? thought Clancy. He noticed the faint mustache on her upper lip.

"We will have to examine the head to see if we can find the bullet. It might have gone clear through and be lost where you found her."

Dr. O'Malley did the usual, making a Y cut with the saw, breaking the rib cage, weighing and examining internal organs. Clancy had seen similar autopsies done a dozen times.

Clancy knew the result, death by shotgun wound. But how close was the perpetrator standing? Dr. O'Malley would know.

"In answer to your question, she was shot at close range."

Once they were finished, the incision was sewn up and the body made as presentable as possible, although the casket would be closed. There was no way the fingers of even the cleverest mortician could disguise the horrible wound Sister Gertrude had sustained. The casket would be sent to the motherhouse in Dublin where a funeral mass, the celebration of Christian burial, would be held. Arrangements would be made by *Lanigans*, of Dublin to convey the body there. Interment would be in Dublin's largest cemetery, *Glashnevin*, not Holy Cross as previously thought.

***

The next day, the Squire read the announcement in the local paper at breakfast. Father Flynn had organized a funeral mass to be said for the soul of Sister Gertrude, in the small parish chapel two days later. All would be welcomed,

"Are you going?" asked Clancy of the Squire. "I'm not too keen on going. She wasn't my favourite person. I don't want to be a hypocrite. So, I will say no."

"I didn't know her so I'm of the same persuasion. Maybe Mansbridge can go in our place and pay our respects."

"Good idea," said the Squire. "I'm not up to it with my ankle

74

the way it is."

***

Later Clancy had second thoughts, deciding he should go to the funeral. Sister Gertrude was unpleasant, but he should keep an eye out for a mourner with a face that didn't fit in. Murderers sometimes like to attend the funerals of their victims.

Near the appointed time, he had Mansbridge call a cab and off he went. It was raining heavily with the mists rising pouring off the land when he took a cab along country roads, through rolling countryside past farms and woods until he arrived at the little stone church with a large silver cross on its steeple. The church looked small, seating for only 200 people at the most.

Clancy stepped out into the cold rain and climbed the steps to the front door. Father Flynn was standing there in his long black cassock. He reached out and shook Clancy's hand. "Thank you for coming. You're one of the few so far. Do go in. I'll wait five minutes more for the stragglers. Tis a sad day for Ireland," he murmured, then bowed his head, but not quick enough to hide the smell of liquor on his breath.

"It's only ten in the morning and already he's been drinking," thought Clancy.

He ducked his head in the doorway and found an empty seat at the back of the church.

One small bouquet of fresh lilies was placed in a brass stand by the altar. A middle-aged woman in a black cloche hat and black coat came forward from a pew and lit tall candles, one on each side of the altar. The service was about to begin.

In the front row were several old ladies with hair held back with black kerchiefs, wearing long wool black coats, crossing themselves and praying. A couple of old men sat beside them. He could see their canes from where he was sitting. One senior sitting in a wheelchair was in the aisle. What Clancy noticed was an absence of youth or the middle-aged. Only the old and decrepit had showed up. None of them looked like a possible murderer.

Father Flynn stepped up to the altar. Everyone was asked to stand. The casket, covered in a green cloth, was wheeled slowly in by middle aged men in black suits, possibly professional mourners. who would ride with the coffin in the hearse afterwards to the Mother House in Dublin. The casket was placed in front of the altar and then everyone sat down.

Father Flynn said a few kind words about Sister Gertrude, her tireless work in the parish, her love for others, and her unfortunate end. "We must not let evil overcome good."

Clancy's eyes wandered. It had been a long time since he'd sat in a church. The stained-glass windows depicted the Stations of the Cross and the suffering of Christ. "We all suffer," thought Clancy "in one way or another." He took time to collect his thoughts and wondered how things were in Mariposa and about Agnes. What would she be doing now?

Father Flynn finished. He went back to the altar, genuflected before the cross, then, taking the chalice up, he blessed the wine and the bread. "Do this in remembrance of Me," he intoned.

The little troop of mourners slowly rose from their pews and went up to the altar. Kneeling on the cushioned bench, they received the body and blood of Christ.

When they were finished, Father Flynn drank the remainder of the wine, wiped the silver chalice with a cloth, and put it and the wafers away in a gold box on the altar. He then picked up the incense burner and swung it over the coffin several times. Making the sign of the cross over the coffin, he commended Sister Gertrude's soul to eternal life.

The service was over. Clancy glanced down at his watch. It had only taken 30 minutes. Clancy slipped out the door, not waiting to talk to anyone, and headed in the direction of the Manor House, hoping some kind soul would give him a lift.

He had walked for about ten minutes in the drizzle, with his hat getting soaked and his feet getting wet when a car pulled up. Father Flynn's head appeared in the window. "Care for a lift? I'm going your way."

"That's grand of you." said Clancy "It is hard to hail a taxi in these parts."

"Have you heard any word on what the Gardai think about who did it?" asked Father Flynn.

"Some hunter, whose gun accidentally went off, is their official version."

The car's windshield wipers whipped back and forth, thunk, thunk.

"I see," said Father Flynn. "Why she went into the woods on her own in hunting season was just plain bad judgment."

"She was determined to go."

"Yes, I heard. Well here we are Clancy, back safe and sound. I'm sure our paths will cross again soon."

"Ta," said Clancy as he got out of the car.

Chapter 12

Bright and early the next day, after a breakfast of scrambled eggs, toast, bacon and hash browns, Clancy decided to revisit the crime scene, to see it again in the daylight to see if he had missed or overlooked anything, left some clue left behind. He followed the tire tracks left there by the Gardai and the ambulance, down the dirt road to the end.

Then he crossed the field. The ground had been mashed up with the tramping of foot prints, smashed branches, and twigs, He headed over to the wood lot, pushed aside the broken branches and found its well beaten path into the centre.

He heard the gurgling stream long before he found it. Then walked along its muddy bank, lined with large slippery stones which were difficult to navigate at times, until he found the large grey Mass Rock lying by the stream.

The yellow police tape still clung to the rock's surface. The ground had been thoroughly tramped around its edges. No clues there. The evening rain had washed away the blood and the rock looked pristine, as if nothing had ever occurred. He stood looking down at it for inspiration. In the stillness, the only sound was the chirping of birds. Large black crows circled overhead.

If this stone could speak, what would it tell me he asked looking down? Sister Gertrude had been shot once in the head from behind. She had been an easy target. There were no trees around the stone to block the view or to hide her from the hunter. Several centuries earlier the open space had been a place for worship, a sacred place for those who had come in secret to practice their faith. Now it was a murder scene. Why choose to murder her here and why now?

Was it because of what she wanted to reveal? Was it because of the discovery of the Mass Rock, or was it because enemies used the opportunity provided by the opening of the hunting season? Was it a good excuse to get rid of her? Were people angry enough to want to kill her? Obviously, she had made someone terribly angry. He looked down at the soil and kicked at the mud. Something shiny caught his eye. A piece of metal. It was Sister Gertrude's silver cross on a silver chain lying in the mud. How had the Gardai missed that? He picked it up and wiped it clean with his handkerchief which he wrapped around the cross. He put in his pocket. He would save this for Father.

What were Sister Gertrude's last thoughts on earth when she'd spied the hunter with his gun. Was it terror? Did she beg for her life? Did she plead for mercy? No, Sister Gertrude would not plead for her life. She was not afraid of anything. It would be hard to instill terror in Sister Gertrude. Did she think that her nun's garb and silver cross would protect her? A shield from evil? Possibly she did.

A man had probably done it. He couldn't picture a woman getting hold of a shot gun. But why now and in such a place? There was a lot of thinking to be done. He looked around again at the clearing. Just then he noticed another path leading away from the rock, going northwards. It was not as heavily trodden on and if he hadn't been looking carefully he would have missed it. He decided to follow it and see where it would take him. This might be the path the killer took. This might be why he and the others had not seen anyone coming or going from the woodlot. He ambled along, pushing aside branches and leaves, tripping over moss covered stones, puddles of water, small pebbles covered with lichen until he came out of the woodlot onto a road.

He looked for signs of a car being parked on the grass or on the gravel. There was one impression of tires on the grass, but not much. It had rained, and the ground was soggy. His gut instinct told him that this was why he had not seen anyone. The killer had left by this path, gone through the woods and gotten back into his parked car and driven off.

A person could come here by car or walk in. But it also could have been neighbours who were in the vicinity. He was not ruling that possibility out.

He walked back to the Manor House, and let himself in. He sat down in the library, with a nice glass of sherry that Mansbridge had given him, put his feet up on the footstool and pondered what he had just seen, rolling the events over and over in his mind. There were a lot of people to interview.

***

While he had the time, he decided to put in another call to the office, to keep himself current on what was going on.

"Things are not so hot," said Greg. "We have an ongoing battle with this hippy with a pony tail, who goes by each morning with his German Shepherd which lifts its leg up when it comes to the fire hydrant near the front door. The smell is excruciating. I've told him to move off and he tells me that you can't control mother nature From Canadian Tire, I've bought cans of spray, but nothing stops it doing its number there. Number one or number two."

"Tell him to get the hell out of there or you'll charge him with mischief. Or else call the Animal Control. Fine him. You're not helpless. How's my cousin's murder investigation going? I forgot to ask you the last time."

"It's coming along. The last report was that they were going over the video tapes from the rear entrance of the building and checking for the time period that she was murdered. They think the killer exited that way."

"Good luck on that. Tapes don't always get a good shot of the face. Has Mira been back?

"Thanks for asking," sneered Greg. "Haven't see her lately, but I'm not holding my breath. Any day now."

Chapter 13

To get some fresh air and oxygen into his brain, he decided to take a walk down to The Crossroads. There he could sit nursing a beer and try to figure out what happened to Sister Gertrude. He realized with a start that he'd been so caught up with the death of Sister Gertrude that he'd momentarily forgotten about Tricia, the Irish hottie. He needed to thank her in an appropriate way for all her generosity in taking him into Cork that day for sightseeing. He looked at his watch. It was short notice, but he'd call her and see if she would like dinner at The Crossroads that evening. What working woman doesn't appreciate being taken out to dinner? A little candlelight, a fire in the grate, lots of wine will get the lady in the right mood for a little romance.

On the first ring Tricia picked up her phone. "Sounds wonderful. Usually I wash my hair on a Monday evening, but I'll put it off and go out with you instead, which is a lot more fun."

He walked back to the Manor House to do some reading and to catch up on things. He was looking forward to his big date that evening and he wanted to be well rested and perky. A short nap was in order. After that he decided to rejoin the Squire in the library to keep him company. He was nursing a sherry when the library door opened. Mansbridge announced, "Dr. Flannery has come to see you to examine your ankle."

"Good. Show him in," said the Squire. "It's about time he came round to check on my ankle. I want a professional opinion on how I'm doing. I want to get up on crutches soon and get going. I've been house bound far too long. Too many things have been happening while I've have been lying here, useless."

"Well how's my patient?" said Dr. Flannery, briefly warming his hands over the grate. "Let me see that ankle of yours. Has it been very painful?" He bent down to slowly unwrap the cloth bandages around the ankle. "It's getting better. Less discolouration. How does it feel? Try to put some weight on it and tell me."

The squire swung his leg onto the floor and pressed his foot down on the carpet. He grimaced. "Still sore."

"We'll send you over some crutches and, in the meantime, keep your feet up."

"Thanks. Like a glass of sherry?"

"Anytime. A glass of sherry is appreciated, day or night." remarked Dr. Flannery," Good for the arteries. Good for the heart."

"You heard what happened to Sister Gertrude?"

"Who hasn't? I am sorry to hear about it. An unfortunate and untimely end."

"More so, since the police believe she was murdered by someone she knew. They don't think she was mistaken for a wild animal by a hunter."

Dr. Flannery raised his eyebrow. "That's a different take on things. I heard that it was a hunting accident."

"Not so. Shot at close range."

"What does that mean?"

"The person knew what he was doing when he shot her. He knew he was shooting Sister Gertrude."

"Who do they think did it?"

"There's a lot of suspects. Everyone who was in the pub that afternoon who heard she was going into the woodlot. It could be anyone."

"What's your opinion of Sister Gertrude? Did she cross your path?" Clancy waited to hear what he had to say.

"Sister Gertrude never minded her own business. That was her big fault. Tried to cause trouble for everyone else, me especially. She gossiped and then tried to get people into trouble. I'll give you an example. Sean's father, the old Squire was dying of cancer of the pancreas. He was on his last days and crazed by pain. He prayed for deliverance, he prayed to die. He called on me to do something about it, to put him out of his misery. I came over and sat by his bedside and had a long chat. What were his wishes? I told him I couldn't do what he asked. It's against the Hippocratic oath, in which I promised to do no harm. I asked him if he wanted t to go into emergency again at the hospital, but he said no. I want to be home when I die. I want to die in my own bed.' The only thing I can give you is a shot of morphine to ease the pain."

"That would help," he said.

"So, I gave him a morphine shot. As everyone knows, too much can cause respiratory failure, in other words, stop your breathing but a small amount is not enough to kill the pain, so one has to choose an amount somewhere in between.

"Unfortunately, an hour later, the Squire's breathing became slower and shallower. Eventually, he stopped breathing altogether. He was dead. I notified his family who had known the end was coming soon. When Sister Gertrude head about it, she called it euthanasia, which is illegal in Ireland. She ferociously complained to the Gardai, but no one paid any attention to her. No charges were ever laid. She was told to mind her own business, that everything she said was libelous.

"So, you see, Sister Gertrude stirred up a lot of trouble. A lot of people had it in for her. I could've gone to jail for the things she claimed I did."

"Did you hear her talk about the Mass Rock that afternoon?" asked Clancy

"I may have, but didn't pay too much attention to her ramblings, that day or any other day. I was in the rear of the pub talking to a group of people."

"Who?" asked Clancy.

"Can't remember. If you'd told me it was important, I would have."

"Well there is a lot of suspects. Anyone around here could have done it."

"By the way," Dr. Flannery turned to address Squire Murphy, "I want to tell you, that I've been taking treatment for prostate cancer. I had surgery and radiation a few years ago, but a Dublin oncologist who I went to see the other day told me that my cancer is progressing to my liver and to my lungs despite everything, chemotherapy and radiation, that has been done for it. There's nothing more that he can do. Usually, old age and natural causes kill men sooner than prostate cancer. I'll have to have Tricia do my house calls when I don't have the strength to do so."

"Well that is a shame. I'm sorry to hear that," acknowledged the Squire. "Very sorry. You've been a long-time friend of the family. You'll be sorely missed."

"Well, I've lived more than three score years and ten. I'm approaching 80 and it's time to pack it in. I am not complaining. It happens to all of us. The Great Reaper comes for everyone."

"Just the same, I've appreciated your care of me, my late wife and my father."

"What more can one say?" thought Clancy, as they silently watched Dr. Flannery close his black medical bag, pick up his jacket, put it on and leave.

***

Clancy went upstairs to his bedroom. He wanted to take extra care with his grooming for his big date with Tricia tonight. Despite his experience and years, he was a little nervous about a date with a much younger woman. He slapped on the aftershave lotion, neatly combed his hair, put on fresh underwear and a pair of cords with a nice crease in them that Mina had ironed for him. He wanted the evening to go well.

He walked down to The Crossroads, a little earlier than the time suggested. Promptly at seven, Tricia pulled in to The Crossroads parking lot and parked her car. Coming into the pub, she looked around for Clancy who was sitting at a table waiting for her.

She looked splendid in a V neck emerald green wool suit. The V neck jacket showed off her generous cleavage. A nice set of pearls showcased her white throat. High heels and a skirt that was thigh-high set off the rest of the outfit.

"Sorry to be a little late."

"No, you're just on time. I am glad that you could make it on such short notice." Clancy got to his feet and gave her a hug. "Here, take a seat next to me by the fire. Have you had a busy day?"

"More or less the usual. I had to give an enema to Paddy Johnson, a farmer whose anatomy was blocked up. I had to be very gentle with his private parts."

"Ouch," exclaimed Clancy. "I hope I don't get blocked. I have very sensitive parts."

"Yes," said Tricia giving him a knowing look, "I hope they're meant to be shared."

Clancy bit his lip. These Irish girls are something else. "I enjoyed so much our trip into Cork, our little excursion the other day. We'd had a bit of excitement, here a bit of bad news." He told her about the finding of the Mass Rock by Mr. Hunter and about Sister Gertrude heading out to find it. "Little did we think anything would happen."

"Tell me about it,", said Tricia leaning in towards him and showing a nice full cleavage, two luscious melons side by side.

"Will do, but first we can relax over a nice bottle of wine. What would you like white or red?"

"Red would be nice. Good for the heart."

"Once we order," said Clancy, picking up the wine list, "how about oysters for starters?

"Sounds great to me."

She patted his hand. "I've been looking forward to this evening all day."

"I'll give our order then tell you all the details." He beckoned Kathleen who was standing behind the bar over. She came and stood by their table, taking her pen and little pad out to write things down.

"Fresh oysters from the sea are a great choice. May I recommend for the main course, the Captain's Seafood platter."

Clancy ordered a dry red wine and fresh oysters for starters. "We'll order the entrees later."

He took his napkin and placed it on his lap, then he noticed Tricia had not taken hers off the table. He reached for it and spread it over her lap.

As he sat back, he said to Tricia, "Sister Gertrude was shot to death right beside the large Mass Rock she found. They think it was a hunter who mistakenly thought she was an animal. But no one has come forward to claim responsibility.

"Last night we had a visit from Father Flynn, concerned that Sister Gertrude's death was near the same spot in the woodlot where Seamus had his accident. Father Flynn wanted to do an exorcism, but the Squire was not in favour of it. Did you know Sister Gertrude well?"

"Not well. She was a first-class busybody, minding everyone else's business, not my type. Too pious for words," Tricia giggled

Thank heavens, thought Clancy upon hearing this. All thoughts of Canada had fled from his mind. Under the table. Tricia had kicked off her pumps and one of her stockinged feet was vigorously rubbing his shoe and ankle back and forth.

This foreplay is better than the meal itself, thought Clancy.

"Another log in the fire?" asked Mr. Cross, coming over to their table with a pleasant smile on his face.

"No, thank you. It's rather warm as it is. Would it be too ungentlemanly if I took off my jacket?"

"Oh, don't stand on ceremony, we're out in the country." said Tricia. She leaned into him. A droplet of sweat appeared in the cleavage, separating those voluminous breasts. A hearty girl that I can get my hands on, thought Clancy, just the kind I like.

"I can tell you an anecdote about Sister Gertrude. Your nephew Seamus wasn't baptized as a baby, something his parents overlooked. It might have been deliberate or just that they were too busy with a new baby. When he died in that accident, Sister Gertrude wanted to deny him a Christian burial. Squire Murphy wasn't too happy about that, nor was his father, Hugh Murphy. Father Flynn overruled her. In the spirit of Pope Francis, Seamus was given a Christian burial."

"That's good to hear. His parents must have been distraught."

Kathleen appeared with a tray of oysters and their wine glasses.

She poured a little wine out for Clancy to sample and asked for his approval.

"Perfect," said Clancy after taking a sip.

Clancy passed the oyster plate to Tricia and then helped himself. "These oysters are slippery." He held one up, leaned his head back and let it slither down his throat. "Down the hatch."

He watched as Tricia lifted a shell and then arched that lovely white neck of hers slowly back.

"Oysters are a great aphrodisiac," he winked at her.

Looking at the main entrée list, Clancy said," the Sea Captain's platter looks good. Scallops, shrimp, mussels, squid, and lobster tails. Put some flesh on your ribs. I like a bonny lass."

Tricia smiled and tipped her glass to his. The wood fire in the grate cast bright shadows across the walls of the room, making it all very warm and cosy. The tall candles flickering on the table added a nice glow. There was only another couple at a table in the far corner. They had the room almost to themselves. "I'm in the mood for romance," thought Clancy.

He felt a warm, soft nose rubbing on his trouser leg. What was it? He glanced down. It was the dog under the table, wanting bits of scrap. "Go away," he whispered to the dog, "get lost. You're not getting any," and he gave it a little kick. The dog whined, jumped out from under the table and went to lie down again in front of the hearth, his head on his paws.

Clancy leaned back, the evening was going well. Would Tricia offer him a nightcap back at her place? Things were looking good in that direction. Her eyes were bright, and her cheeks were glowing. Things were progressing at a horse's gallop not a donkey's trot.

Then it was dessert time, some chocolate sticky pudding, loaded with calories and thick whipped cream on top with Irish coffee to finish the dinner.

"I can't drink too much, or I won't be able to drive," protested Tricia, giggling. "Easy does it," she giggled, leaving a little wine in the bottom of her glass.

Tricia settled back in her chair, folded up her napkin and sighed a long sigh. "It's so difficult for me to say this, Clancy."

"Try me," said Clancy eagerly leaning forward to hear her.

Her red fingernail traced back and forth on the hairs of the back of his hand. "It's very difficult. I'm basking in the afterglow of this wonderful dinner."

"Let yourself go. Let your feelings flow," said Clancy. "Don't hold nothing back."

"This was delicious." She smiled at him. "I've enjoyed myself thoroughly."

There was a pause. Clancy's ears were pointed.

"Let me give you a ride back to the Manor house. I'm a working girl and have to get up bright and early tomorrow morning. Too early to linger and savour the moment, otherwise I'd have you up to my place for a nightcap. I can't ask you back tonight."

He touched her thigh with his knee. She didn't move away. "I'll be glad to take a rain cheque anytime." He raised her hand to his lips and kissed it. Then he stood up and gave her a big kiss on those lovely red lips before she picked up her purse to leave.

"Then that's settled. A rain cheque it is."

Chapter 14

"Oh, what a beautiful morning," thought Clancy after he woke up from a long, deep sleep the next day. He had enjoyed himself immensely the prior evening. Good things were promised ahead. He took his time getting up, getting dressed and then having breakfast downstairs. The Squire was busy reading the Irish Independent newspaper.

"Sleep well?"

"Yes, like a log. I had a nice evening out with Tricia Busker, a charming young woman."

"She seems like a very capable young woman."

"Very capable. Going to stretch my legs, get some fresh air."

"Do that."

***

Clancy strode down the road to the pub. A truck carrying milk cans lumbered by on its way to the dairy. This was followed by a tractor pulling a wagon of hay. Clancy waved. The farmer waved back at him. Busy today he thought.

He strode up to the bar thinking that it was too bad he couldn't spend his whole career conducting investigations in a pub, much more pleasant than his dinky office back in Mariposa. "Pour me a pint of Guinness will you love? I'm a thirsty man. Just walked up from the Manor House. I'm not as young as I use to be. Long in the tooth. Not young and frisky like you." This wasn't quite true, for this morning he felt very frisky and energetic.

"You look pretty perky to me," said Kathleen, placing a beer mat on the bar for his drink.

"How did a pretty girl like you end up at The Crossroads? I thought the young and restless would either be gone to Cork or Dublin."

"Well, it's easy to explain. I got my O levels and then my A levels. I could have gone on to university but there wasn't the money and I didn't have high enough marks for a scholarship. There are not many jobs available. Mr. Cross offered me this and I took it. I'm saving up my money to go on a trip and see the world."

"Sensible girl," said Clancy.

He looked around the room to see if he knew anyone. There were few patrons, just old, retired farmers sitting at tables in the back. "Haven't seen Lucy around lately. Where has she been these last couple of days, Kathleen?"

Kathleen, who had been polishing the copper handles of the kegs, looked up, "She's recovering from her recent break up with Edward Murphy."

"Oh, she was going around with him, was she?"

"Lucy use to go out with the other brother, Seamus, before his terrible accident. After he died she was devastated. But with the passage of time she pulled herself together. Then Edward showed an interest. He's the second oldest brother. They've been going out to dances, fiddlers' concerts and Celtic musical evenings held in the pub. She'd been with him ever since. She and Edward went to primary school together. They're the same age. Then, in her teens, her parents sent her to convent school to keep her away from boys. That didn't work. I think convent school, with all those nuns telling you not to dance too close, makes girls in the end boy crazy. Lucy has rotten luck when it comes to boy friends."

"Why do you say that?" asked Clancy.

Just then, a farmer in muddy boots who Clancy didn't recognize came through the door and stood at the bar. "A Guinness."

"Coming right up." She let the foam settle before she handed him his drink, and then waited while he found a chair near the fire before turning back to Clancy.

"Here's to your health." Clancy lifted his glass, nodded at the stranger, and then took a sip. It was warm, room temperature, not cold like Canadian beer.

Kathleen leaned in closely and whispered. "After going out with him for a year, she thought it was time he proposed, get serious, declare his intentions, like put a ring on her finger. This is all village gossip, you realize. When he was not forthcoming she broke off with him.

"The break up hit her hard, even though she was the one who called it off for reasons, I will explain to you. I shouldn't be telling you this, but I know that you will keep it confidential. There is no one around to overhear us, but I think Edward is a real cad. Lucy confided in me, and I know you will keep it confidential.

"Can you hold on a sec, I'll get back to you, but I have got to wipe down that table over there and pick up the condiments." Kathleen picked up a damp cloth and headed over.

"Sure thing," said Clancy.

Kathleen returned to the bar. "I don't want it to get out, but Lucy was two months pregnant. When she found she was pregnant, she confronted Edward. He told her that he wasn't sure he was the father. She said then who else could it be, a ghost? You're the only one that I've been going out with. He then told her point blank that he wasn't going to marry her."

"What were his reasons?" asked Clancy. "She's a very pretty girl."

"He said he was too young to be tied down with a family and wasn't keen on children. He had no savings, nothing set aside for the future. He didn't even have a real job. It was her problem, not his. She came crying to me for help.

"I told her, book an appointment with old Doc Flannery. He's very sympathetic.

"She had several choices. Did she want to keep the baby? If she kept the baby, she would be a single mother and have to bring it up on her own which would be a bit of a struggle financially. Edward wouldn't lift a finger. She could have the baby adopted or her third choice was to have an abortion. It's hard to get an abortion in Ireland.

"When she went to Doc Flannery he suggested that if she didn't want to keep the baby she should consider having a D and C within the next couple of days and then stay off work for a few days."

"A 'D & C'? I haven't heard of that one."

"Dilation and curettage of the womb. Women get it done for irregular bleeding. It's scraping and cleaning up the womb. So that is what she did. He did the D & D which is legal. She now just has to pull her shoulders back and get on with her life. It's hard to do that at first. I hope she gets over her heartache with Edward and puts that relationship behind her."

Kathleen paused to pick up a glass and polish it with her tea towel. Just then, the Jack Russell terrier came running around the corner of the bar and jumped up at Clancy's knee. Clancy reached down to pat it but at the same time pushing it away from his trousers. "I have a dog like this at home. They're very affectionate."

"I'll tell you another thing," said Kathleen, "that nun, Sister Gertrude, got wind of the operation that was done in Doc Flannery's office. Either the secretary or the nurse gossiped about the D & C. Sister Gertrude said that what Doc Flannery did was really abortion and illegal. That old bitch was sniffing around, causing trouble, not minding her own business throwing it in Lucy's face. It's amazing how she snoops around and finds out things."

"What a shame," said Clancy and, to change the subject, said, "I hear Sabrina is going out with Edward's brother, Quincy."

"If she is, I don't know what she sees in him. He hasn't a reputation for working hard or applying himself. The romance will probably fizzle out. It will be just like his brother's."

"You heard what happened to Sister Gertrude?"

"Yes, news travels fast. She was just in here that afternoon and now she's dead."

"Are you surprised?"

"A little. But Sister Gertrude was not popular."

"Oh? I'm sorry to hear that," said Clancy, sipping slowly on his pint, waiting to hear what she would have to say next.

"She was blackmailing everybody. She had it in for everybody. Sister Gertrude stirred up a lot of trouble. A lot of people had it in for her."

"Did Sister Gertrude ever show a nice side?"

"They say she was very pleasant when collecting money to repair the roof of the church, or for money to buy floral arrangements to decorate the altar at mass. Yes, she was ever so nice when asking for money. Otherwise she was busy causing trouble."

"I can see that. The police think it was personal and there are a lot of suspects. If you hear anything, Kathleen, please let me know. You know I'll keep everything you told me confidential. Now to finish my pint and go outside to catch some sun. Thanks for the information."

Clancy was feeling mellow, catching the last of the sunny days at a picnic table set outside the front door of the pub, watching the cars drive by. The weather was similar to Canada's only a bit warmer, thanks to the Gulf Stream. A car's horn sounded.

***

"Hello there." Tricia was leaning out of her car window as she drove into the parking lot.

"Top of the morning to you, Tricia." Clancy was proud that he was wearing his cloth cap like the country squire, so that he would blend in as one of the locals.

"Yes," she said, smiling, "it's a great day. Wonderful dinner last night, it was. I was just going to drop in for a quick drink. I'll park my car in the parking lot and then join you. How's the Squire these days?"

"He's just taking it easy. He'll need physiotherapy for his ankle in order to get back to walking, but otherwise he is quite chipper."

"That reminds me. I should drop in to see him, to see how he's coming along."

"Do that. Come for morning coffee. It's served around 10 a.m. along with some nice ginger biscuits that the housekeeper makes."

"How are things going for you? How's the sleuthing coming along?"

"I've been visiting various people, chatting to people, the usual. The Squire asked me to do a bit of investigating."

"Not much of a vacation for you, coming all this way from Canada."

"Oh, I'm enjoying myself never the less. I'm lucky to have met such good company."

Clancy found a nice table by the fire and pulled up a comfortable chair for Tricia. Then he went up to the bar where Kathleen was on duty. "A Guinness," he said. "And then I'll wait for my lady friend to order."

Tricia, all smiles, burst into the room and sat down beside him. "You'll have to come over to my place tomorrow for that nightcap I promised you. I won't be working Saturday and I can relax. There's a lot of driving in this job, to visit patients in their homes. I spend hours on the road, but I love my patients, they're so grateful for my care. Sometimes they give me a little thank you present. Sometimes it's just a nice cup of tea. This morning, I visited a woman who had just given birth to a healthy baby daughter, assisted by the midwife. She was tired but happy. I gave her breastfeeding instructions. So, Friday night, it is."

"Sounds really nice Tricia. I'd love to come."

"Then it's on. I hate to leave you." said Tricia getting to her feet. "I just stopped by to give you the invitation. Can't stay for a drink. I would love to sit here and gab, but I have another appointment with Paddy Green, an alcoholic, in about twenty minutes and a fair drive to get there. He's a man who loves to drink more than he likes to eat." Then she was out the door.

"Well, all the best, take care," said Clancy, sorry to see her go.

He sipped at his drink. He was the only one around. There was no one to talk to. While he was mulling things over, and with time on his hands, he called the office in Mariposa.

The line was very scratchy. "Greg, your voice still sounds funny. Are you under strain? It sounds so far away."

"Since you last called, things have been stressful. The toilet overflowed. Someone threw something down the toilet. The place smelled like a sewer and there was a lot of mopping up to do. I had to keep the windows open all the time to get fresh air. We couldn't get much work done because it was so cold in the office. The plumber had to come, and you know what plumbers charge.

"Then your friend, Mira, dropped by for a little friendly chat, putting her hands on my tie and stroking it, trailing her fingers along my arm, wanting information. She was so close to me that anyone walking by in the hall or looking through the front window would think we were having sexual intercourse. This would be construed as behavior unbecoming to a police officer and I would get blamed. I was breathing so heavily I thought I'd pass out. She wheedled out of me where you were and got the Squire's number."

"The Squire's number," yelled Clancy, then looking around in case someone overheard him shout. "How easily you caved. What did she promise you? A leg over? Stop being a pussy, Greg. Get out your baton."

"Get out my what? My what? I can't hear you."

"Your baton. What do you think I said? Use it." And he hurriedly rung off.

Thinking of home, Clancy wondered what Agnes had been up to. Agnes liked being a housewife and not working. She had been in data processing for fifteen years, not a people friendly job. He knew her routine pretty well. In the morning, getting dressed in her blue pantsuit and trainers, she would drive down to the park, then walk along the boardwalk by the lake, which she claimed was so invigorating with the fresh breezes blowing inland. It was fall now. The boat slips in the harbor would be empty, the vessels in winter storage. There was a narrow piece of landfill, jutting out into the harbor covered with bush and shrubs, where the sea gulls liked to stand on the cement pilings. They were still plentiful. Then there was the wonderful view across the lake where, in summer, the camps of various organizations, the YMCA Geneva Park was one example, came to life. Afterward Agnes would meet her buddies, Sally and Grace, for morning coffee at Apple Annie's or a quick lunch at Mariposa Market, a soup and sandwich, when it wasn't too crowded, then an afternoon of bingo at the legion if it were raining, or, in good weather, weeding and straightening up the garden, trimming the hedge, raking the leaves, things he usually did. Or at least, things Agnes sometimes corralled him into doing.

Yes, Agnes could easily fill up her days. He didn't want to rattle her cage or upset the apple cart, so to speak. It was better not to phone.

***

Clancy eased himself up to the bar to sit comfortably on a high stool. Then he rested his feet on the foot rung below. This kind of investigation, visiting the pub on a daily basis to get information was a pleasant experience. It agreed with him. It was true he was neglecting his sightseeing. But this was much more interesting.

He was pleased to see that Lucy the blond-haired pony tailed Colleen with freckles on her arms and nose was back behind the bar. She was a pretty sight to see and much too pretty to be moping around at home. He ordered a pint.

"Nice to see you again. Haven't seen you around much."

"I wasn't feeling so good lately."

"Better now?"

"Much better." She lowered her eyes and blushed. "I broke off with my boy friend, Edward." She threw her arms in the air, "I'm free as a bird." She paused, with a painful look in her eyes. "This was my second serious relationship that's ended." She leaned forward on the bar and stared into his face, "Do you think I'm unlucky in love?"

"You're too pretty and too young to say that," said Clancy.

Lucy's blushed, her cheeks burned. She held out her hands. "Look at my fingers. No ring, no future."

"Many a frog you kiss, before you kiss a prince. Plenty of fish in the sea, my dear. If I was a young man, I'd snatch you up in a minute."

"How kind of you to say that. I'll have to get my hook baited with a nice, fat, juicy worm."

Clancy took another sip of his pint. "You heard what happened to Sister Gertrude while you were away."

"Yes, Kathleen told me. Sister Gertrude had met a dreadful end, shot in the head by a hunter, out in the woodlot. I'm not surprised, but I wouldn't wish it on anyone.

"She may have been in Holy Orders, but she was a first class bitch She had very strong views on the catechism and Catholic dogma. I'm surprised she dressed in modern fashion rather than wearing the old black habit, and wimple. I've tried to keep clear of her, but I haven't been always successful. "Lucy blushed a crimson red. Clancy knew from his conversation with Kathleen what she was implying. She stared hard at him. "Are you surprised at my comments? I hope I don't sound bitter."

"Not at all. Quite a few people think the same as you do."

Just then, Trip, the dog, bounced around the corner, wagging its tail, barking and sniffing at Clancy's crotch. "Down boy, down." And he brushed the dog off his legs. "Friendly dog."

"Yes. What a shame about Sister Gertrude. It's strange she was all alone in the woods, looking for a Mass Rock."

"It was her idea to go there. We couldn't persuade her not to go. Have you heard anything? Any gossip in the pub?"

"Not a thing, quiet as the night."

"Any ideas as to who did it?"

"No, I thought it was hunters. But it could be anyone in the neighbourhood."

Lucy wiped the counter off and set out beer mats.

"There will be a curse on that stone now. It's hard to believe Sister Gertrude is dead. We are all in shock. It must be hard on Father Flynn to understand how a sister, a nun, could be murdered, but," she added, "Father Flynn has his own peccadilloes. He's overly friendly with young girls. His other problem is that he drinks the leftover wine after communion, which all the priests do, but this has got him started, I fear, on the road to becoming an alcoholic. But he is liberal in his thinking, compassionate and kind. The same couldn't be said for Sister Gertrude."

"If you hear anything let me know."

"Will do. I'm staying with farmer, Jim Muir. He has an empty house after his wife up and left him for another man in the village. I've never met her, but I gather she was a real bitch. He's a lot older than me. People will think I have a father complex, but I don't. It's just a temporary arrangement, not permanent."

"As long as you're happy and it works for you."

"If you'll excuse me, I have to go and put the glasses through the dishwasher." Trip perked up his ears, then shot around the corner of the bar to the kitchen, following in her footsteps.

Clancy settled back to drink his pint. Who hated Sister Gertrude enough to kill her? Would he have to interview half the village? No, it would be those in the pub who knew that she would be in the woodlot, the ones who heard her make the announcement. He settled back and took another sip of his beer and tried to figure out who was in the pub that afternoon.

Ping, ping went his phone. Clancy picked it up but didn't recognize the number. Who could be calling him from Canada?

He gave a cautious, "Hello."

"It's Mira from the Mariposa Packet."

"Mira?" He swore under his breath. "How the hell did you get my phone number? This is a private line." He knew already what Greg had done, but he'd said he'd given the Squire's number, not his private number. Mira would stop at nothing to get news for the Mariposa Packet. What happened? How did she get hold of it?

"Well Greg's been very helpful in the past. So, I leaned on him. He caved in pretty quickly. He's never been known to keep his cards too close to his chest."

"Your tactics could land you in jail," said Clancy, "it's called skullduggery. I hate to imagine what you promised him in exchange for the information."

"Sorry about that. Truly sorry." She didn't sound sorry. "Greg told me that you were investigating a murder that happened on the Squire's property, a nun got her head blown off. That's big news. Are you close to solving it? We could run a story with the caption, *Clancy's work never ceases, a murder follows him wherever he goes, another dead body found on his vacation, which he is trying to solve.* How about that?"

"Mira, I would like to remind you that I'm on vacation and that my time is my own. I'm not answerable to anyone."

"Nonsense," said Mira. "In his heart a copper is never off duty, never at leisure, no matter where he is."

"You can't call in any favours from me, Mira. There are no inducements," said Clancy. "There are no IOUs. No pillow talk, no leg over. I'm immune to your forms of bribery."

"I was hoping you'd appreciate this call from your side of the Atlantic. Obviously, you don't. I'm a night hawk, not an early bird but I got up early to make this call, with the five-hour difference. Thanks, but no thanks."

"Oh, Mira, you'll get your reward in heaven. Not here, unfortunately, down on earth. It's nice to know that you're still breathing fire and brimstone. Got to go." Feeling irritated and out of sorts, he hung up. It was time to head back to the Manor House.

Another elaborate dinner was served in the dining room. It was getting chilly in this long wood paneled room, so Mansbridge came and put a log on the fire. This time Clancy noticed the entree was fresh lamb produced on the farm, with mint jelly, boiled potatoes with parsley and brussels sprouts.

He was sitting at the end of the long table opposite the Squire, which didn't help for conversation, you had to shout to be heard, but that was okay. But with Mansbridge at his elbow to pass the side dishes and condiments and several glasses of wine and a good meal, who needed conversation? Afterwards the Squire said he was going to do some reading in the library.

Clancy went upstairs for a good night's sleep. The room was still warm from the fire in the grate. He opened the casement window for some fresh air, then climbed into bed under a thick, warm quilt.

He fell into a sound sleep but, in the midst of a dream, he awoke. Someone was walking around, either outside in the hall or downstairs. He sat up in bed with sweat on his brow. The sound was coming from downstairs. He heard the creak of the floorboards. Someone was walking around in slippered feet on the wooden floor downstairs. He thought quickly about the Squire. It can't be him. Thankfully, for the last two nights, he had been able to climb the stairs to sleep in his own bed.

Clancy slipped out of bed, grabbed his flashlight from the bureau and went and stood behind the door with his arm raised ready to pounce. The footsteps began coming slowly up the stairs. Then paused. Clancy held his breath ready to spring. But the footsteps stopped, then retreated. Clancy waited until the sounds of footsteps died altogether, then put the flashlight down and got back into bed. He made a mental note to check the stairs in the morning.

At breakfast, he waited for the Squire to bring up the topic of hearing a possible prowler in the night. He didn't mention it. He might not have heard, being too fast asleep. Clancy decided to say nothing, and to just wait and see.

***

Clancy was sitting in the sun outside The Crossroads when

he heard the toot of a horn. Tricia leaned out of her car window.

"I have some time over lunch hour and then some. How about I drive back after I finish with my patients and we go into Cork, for lunch. It's not far. I know an interesting pub, The Franciscan Well Brewery and Beer Pub down on the Quai.

"That sounds good to me," said Clancy.

He had been waiting just a few minutes when she pulled in. Promptly at one, Tricia was in The Crossroads parking lot ready to pick him up.

"A nice sunny day, the sun has burned off the morning mist and fog," said Clancy.

He got in the passenger seat. In the interim, her driving hadn't improved one bit. As before, she drove like a maniac, so fast that he could not see over the top of the hedgerows when they went around curves. Clancy was thrown against her, even though he was wearing a seat belt. He couldn't see the traffic coming towards him, Clancy would never have taken the risks she did.

They were coming around one curve and a truck was in their path coming towards them, blocking the way. Tricia jumped on the brakes and the car skidded to a halt.

"Close call," said Clancy wishing he was a praying man.

"No, not really." said Tricia, carelessly

Around another curve, they had to stop for a flock of pheasants boldly crossing the road.

"It's hunting season. They don't know it yet, but they're going to end up on somebody's dinner table tonight," said Clancy, chuckling to himself.

"This pub is kind of hard to find. It's in the North Mall down by Popes Quai, off the R847, not far from the Cork Opera House. It was built on the site of an old Franciscan monastery, hence the name. It has a micro brewery inside making craft beer. Would you like a brewery tour?"

"Nah, I have had enough of tours, just sit me down with a nice cold one."

"Inside there's a large bar," continued Tricia," Outside there's a courtyard with its own wood fire pizza oven."

They drove over the bridge and into the city centre. finding a parking space close to the pub.

Clancy noticed how nice Tricia looked,

She was dressed casually but trendily. She was wearing well pressed jeans and a black blazer, a white shirt unbuttoned to show ample cleavage and, on her bare feet, penny loafers.

Outside, the pub looked like a holy well site. Not that he had visited any.

"Find a comfortable place for us to sit, Tricia you choose."

"How about the courtyard since it's a sunny day?" said Tricia. "I suggest we order Pompeii pizza which is one of their specialties. You choose one of their craft beers. The waiter will help you to decide."

The place was so popular with the noon crowd from nearby offices that it was hard at first to find a seat. Finally, they got a table, settled in and waited for their order. Under the table, Tricia rubbed his foot with her shoe.

Seagulls from the quay were shrieking "Ca,ca", wheeling and circling the sky then quickly diving down for a crust of bread dropped on the pavement. Some perched on nearby chairs, waiting.

"I was hoping we could have a little chat," said Tricia her nails raking gently the inside of his palm.

Clancy's ears perked up. What was she going to suggest?

"I need a policeman's opinion. You know Sabrina. She came into work the other day with a black eye. When I questioned her about it, she said she'd bumped into a door." Tricia rolled her eyes. "How lame can you get"

Clancy bit his lip. "Yeah, it does sound a bit off."

"What do you think? I think her boyfriend gave it to her."

Clancy nodded. "Could be, could be."

"I don't know who he is. She never told me. She's very secretive about her new romance."

Clancy thought the best thing that he could do was play dumb. It must be Quincy. He'd seen the couple together on an outdoor patio in Cork on his last visit.

"I wouldn't encourage the relationship. It sounds abusive."

"Yes, you're so right. I don't want to be intrusive but if she shows up with a broken rib or a broken arm, then I'll call the Gardai."

"That's a good idea," said Clancy.

The pizza was delicious, one of the best he'd tasted. The beer wasn't half bad. It was nice to try something new and different.

The ride home was pretty much the same, Tricia driving like a maniac and Clancy falling against her soft, warm body.

Chapter 15

After breakfast, Clancy decided to do more reading. He headed to the library to read through more of the genealogy and biographies of the Murphy clan. It was interesting. They hadn't been angels. There had been a poacher who had hunted for pheasants on the Squire's land and fished for salmon in his streams, but he too was eventually caught and hanged, to be found by one of his children. It was rough justice, meted out, and quickly enforced. Once caught, he'd been strung up on a neighbouring tree like a rabbit, albeit no trial, no mercy.

In the Independent Times, he'd read that it was believed that there hadn't been a serial killer in Ireland until, in 2015, a book on Kieran Kelley, the Irish vagrant came out. In it he confessed to pushing fifteen people onto the London Underground tracks. He claimed he had stood next to them on the platform and then gave them a push. The police weren't suspicious. When they investigated and asked for witnesses, he stepped forward and said he stood next to persons who jumped. He claimed that they were suicidal. The case was too hard to prosecute so he was jailed for another offense. No hanging for him.

Mansbridge knocked on the door, "Sergeant Finney is here to see you."

I wonder why he needs to talk to me thought Clancy.

Sargent Finney, a tall slim man in his early forties, was standing in the hall holding his hat. He nodded at the Squire and directly addressed Clancy. "It's you I want to speak to. I know that you told me you were only going to take two weeks away from your job in Canada. You only have one and half weeks to go."

"Yes, that's right. I don't want to overstay my welcome." Clancy glanced over at the Squire.

"We need your help. We're short staffed and can't handle all the work. We need an outsider's opinion. Also, you and the Squire were the last to see Sister Gertrude alive. During our inquiries we found that she'd made herself quite a few enemies There are so many suspects.

"Do you think you could contact your home office and ask for an extension, one week, tops? It's a big favour to us. We really need your help. We'll arrange for financial compensation for your time if that's a problem.

"There's not enough evidence, at this point in time, to prepare a case for the prosecution. We'll do follow up on your suggestions after you leave. The point of my call is that we'd like to have your thoughts on a suspect before you head back to Canada."

Clancy sighed, of course he would help. "I am very flattered that you could use my help. I didn't want to butt in, in a foreign country, foreign soil so to speak. The compensation that you mentioned sounds interesting. Your euro is high now, higher than the Canadian dollar. It would come in handy.

"What I'll do is to notify the office to see if they can spare me. which I'm pretty sure they can. If there's no problem, then I will stay over." Of course, the office could spare him.

"I appreciate your help in these matters." Sergeant Finney gave a nod to the Squire and Clancy and then left the room.

Clancy turned to the Squire. and asked what he thought about the fact that the Gardai wanted him to stay another week to help out in their investigation? They wouldn't necessarily be making an arrest based on his observations, but they would gather evidence in the case. At least he could tell them where to look.

"Another week?" said the Squire musing. "My ankle is still not up to par. I can hardly get around at all, You're very good company, Clancy. I 'm glad to have you here. It's wonderful to have you around while I'm laid up."

"I don't want to put you to any trouble or expense. I could go and stay at The Crossroads. They have upstairs bedrooms to rent."

"Nonsense," said the Squire. "I'm a lonely man in a big house. Having you stay here, it's no trouble at all. Think nothing of it. It's settled."

It was no problem for him to stay another week. He loved being waited on in luxurious surroundings with no responsibilities, like walking the dog, raking the leaves, etc. that he would have to do at home. Agnes had a never-ending list of things she wanted done.

***

He next put in a call to the office in Canada. The line, as usual, was not too clear. He recognized Greg's voice. "Greg, are there any ongoing emergencies at the office?"

"Oh, we're doing nothing over here, just twiddling our thumbs, drinking coffee and making paper airplanes. That guy's dog is still pissing on the hydrant outside the front door. I'll catch him and his dog in the act one of these days and then it'll be shish-ka-bob."

"Don't be so sarcastic. In that case, you'll have to hold the fort another week. I've been asked to stay a bit longer. The Gardai need my help, they're short staffed. I knew you wouldn't mind."

"There's a lot of paper work that's piling up on your desk and I'm not doing it."

"I'll look after it when I get back. By the way, Mira contacted me. I suppose you know all about that and how she got my number."

"Oh, she did, did she? I wasn't aware"

"Bullshit. Bullshit. You gave it to her."

"Me?" squealed Greg.

"Yes, you. Any murders?"

"No, it's been peaceful since you left."

"Anyway, what about my cousin's murder in Toronto?"

"They got the time frame matched it against the exit door's security camera and they came up with a picture of a twenty-five-year-old, black male, dressed in jeans and hoodie, 6 feet tall, living in the Jane Finch area. Because of the use of carding which the police force and the government are planning to discontinue, they were able to get his name, and where he lived. They haven't got his exact address, but they have a name.

"In a way, the victim brought it on herself. She didn't know him, and she just buzzed him in. She should have checked the screen in the lobby. Most of her clients were older men, middle aged and older, men that she could handle if there were any difficulties. But, on blind faith, she lets this stranger up to her apartment without checking. And he pushed his way in. She must have mistakenly thought it was a client she was waiting for.

"Or the other scenario is she just heard a knock on the door. Thinking it was her client, who usually comes at that time, let him in. When he came through the door, she realized, too late, her mistake. He probably put his foot in the door and forced his way in.

105

They believe robbery was the motive, but they don't know for sure. Anyway, he ended up stabbing her and leaving by the rear exit, thinking he'd left no trail behind him. Fingerprints and the security video will convict him. Rather neat sleuthing, huh?"

"I'll get back to you," said Clancy. "I have a lot on my plate."

***

The phone went ping, ping again. Now who could can that be? He looked at the number. It was long distance from Canada. The number looked familiar. He tried to jog his memory.

"Hello, hello."

"Hello stranger." said a sultry voice. "It's me, Mira. I got up early to phone you. I hear that you're helping the Gardai solve that murder of the nun. Will you use prayer as your inspiration?"

"It's you, isn't it? I thought as much. Who told you that the Gardai wanted my help?"

"A little bird," said Mira.

"I bet dollars to doughnuts, it was a big bird called Greg."

"A journalist never reveals her sources."

"I will deal with Greg when I get back. Cut to the chase. What do you want, Mira?"

"I need some material for a story I'm working on. Clancy Murphy, innocent abroad, stumbles on another murder. More details, Clancy. Who are the suspects? Was she pregnant when she was murdered? Was she secretly in love with the young village priest and confessed that he'd made her pregnant? Did she linger too long with the church deacon in the vestibule? Or the organist for that matter? There's a lot happening in the choir loft these days and it's not just singing. There are all kinds of possibilities. Spare nothing. Out with it."

"Mira, I'm tight as a clam when it comes to you. No amount of digging will pry me open."

"Oh, don't be like that. We're buddies from the same home town. Doesn't loyalty count at all? We Canadians should stick together."

"Give me a break," said Clancy as he hung up.

Now, the most important phone call to his wife Agnes, who would not be too pleased about the change of plan. She hadn't wanted him to come over to Ireland in the first place. He wasn't too keen to hear her objections about his having to extend his stay.

Her voice sounded anxious. "Why are you calling? Have you

106

been in an accident? Are you alright? In good health? No bones broken?"

"Perfectly fine and you, Honey? I don't know how to tell you this, but, I have to stay an extra week to help the police over here. I don't want to, but they're short staffed and need my help."

"We miss you. Everyone misses you. You do have responsibilities at home. You have a family."

"It can't be helped. I'm needed here."

"You're needed at home. You have family responsibilities. The grass needs cutting. The dog needs to be walked. We have to arrange for the storm windows to be put on. The furnace needs to be checked before winter comes. The carbon monoxide and smoke detectors have to have fresh batteries. The chimney should be cleaned. The lawn furniture has to be dragged in and put away in the basement. There are a thousand and one things to do before winter comes."

"Yes, I know. Well it won't be long. The week will fly by. I'll make it up to you. Not much else is happening. Pretty boring otherwise. Love you." He rung off thinking thank heavens I'm not there. I need the vacation. Besides, every time I want sex, I feel I have to sit up and beg for it, like a dog. A good dog gets a bone, I get sex and bad dogs get none.

He put his phone back in his jacket pocket. He was glad that he was here in Ireland, not back home.

Secretly loving the lifestyle at a Manor house complete with a butler serving unlimited amount of sherry, beer and wine, Clancy was relieved. He didn't really want to move out. That was the last thing he wanted. Once you get use to the high life, it's hard to shift your sights downward.

Chapter 16

"Going down to the pub," said Clancy to Mansbridge. "Be back in about an hour."

He headed out the door, but his way down the road was blocked by a flock of sheep. The farmer acted very nonchalantly when Clancy tried to wade through the moving bodies. "My good man," cried out Clancy, impatiently, to the farmer, "I need to get through."

"Oh, is that the problem?"

The farmer blew on his whistle and his dog, with his ears pointed, started barking at the sheep herding them back and forth. The sheep obeyed, moving over to the side of the road.

"Ta," said Clancy.

With a hop and a skip, he was soon down the road to the pub. He stepped inside and headed towards the fireplace, shaking off the cool morning air by placing his hands before a roaring log fire burning in the grate. "Cold morning," he said, nodding at the men who were standing around the fire drinking pints. They returned his nod. A couple of men had their heads bent over a checkerboard, pondering their next moves. Clancy watched them for a few minutes then he headed over to the pub owner, Mr. Cross who was standing behind the bar putting the cost of a meal into the cash register. Beside him was a pile of paper slips that he had to put through. Clancy waited until he'd finished.

"You know most of the gossip about what goes on around here, Mr. Cross. Did anyone from the pub mention they were going hunting the other day, the day that Sister Gertrude was killed?"

"No, I didn't hear anyone saying that they were going out specifically to hunt. But most farmers know it's hunting season. It is just the first couple of days."

"Can you recall who was in the pub that afternoon?"

"Quite a few people. Several neighbouring farmers, Doc Flannery, Mr. Hunter, Sister Gertrude, Jim Muir, Edward and Quincy. I can't remember them all. It was a busy afternoon."

Well, that's a start thought Clancy

"Did you see anyone leave about the same time that Sister Gertrude did?"

"I saw someone drive out of the parking lot in a red Volkswagen about that time. Is that any help?"

"Could be, everything helps. The Gardai want my assistance in this case. They're short staffed."

"They do, do they? Well, best of luck."

Chapter 17

When Clancy got back to the Manor House, he had a nice glass of sherry and a beer with lunch of pickled eggs, pickles, bread and cheese which had been spread out on the sideboard. A little nap was then in order before he set out again. No rest for the wicked.

"I'm off to the pub to continue my investigations," he told Mansbridge. It sounded so high minded. This was more fun than doing boring investigating work in Mariposa. How he would miss these investigative pub sessions when he got back home.

This time, when he walked down the road, a farmer's truck hauling hay was slowly moving up the road, blocking his way. He had to wait patiently until it passed.

The pub this afternoon was more crowded. He looked over to the group standing with their backs to the fire. It included Doc Flannery, Father Flynn and Quincy. He walked over to them and grandly announced, "I've been asked to stay another week to help out the Gardai investigation the death of Sister Gertrude. They're having a hard time finding any suspects. No witnesses have come forward."

"I don't think you'll get much help from the public. Sister Gertrude was not popular," said Doc Flannery, shaking his head. "Not popular at all."

"Sad to say, I agree," said Father Flynn, taking another sip of beer," no one is crying in their beer about her demise. At the mass I held for her soul, you were there, Clancy, you could see only about ten people showed up and that's not many for these parts."

"What do you think, Quincy?" asked Clancy

"I thought that she was mean and downright miserable. One shouldn't speak ill of the dead, but she was. Deny it." Quincy took a big sip of his beer.

"I found a road north of the woodlot. Did any of you see anyone on that road that day? Apparently, it's hardly used. No homes on it, just farmland."

The men shook their heads, "We were all in here, having a pint," said Doc Flannery.

"I went visiting the sick afterwards." said Father Flynn.

"And I was doing chores after having a pint in here," said Quincy.

Clancy realized after talking to the group that he had to separate the members and have a one to one chat. Otherwise things would be muddled, and he wouldn't find out anything.

Chapter 18

Clancy decided that after lunch he should interview Hugh Murphy, the Squire's brother. He might have seen something, someone coming or going that day. On the other hand, he might not. Also, he figured that he might have some opinion about Sister Gertrude since she'd protested about allowing his son to have a Christian burial. Were there lingering feelings of animosity? Would he have acted on those feelings?

He decided to phone first to make sure that Hugh was not out working in the fields.

"Yes, I'll be glad to see you. You'll be just in time for afternoon tea and coffee."

Clancy called a cab which took twenty minutes to arrive. He'd get needed exercise if he walked, but he wasn't keen on walking. Murphy's farm was several farms away on the main road. It was a beautiful day. As he waited along the roadside he could see buttercups, evening primrose, and garlic mustard growing in the ditches beneath the hedges. At the edge of the field, bumble bees hovered over dandelions, oxeye daisies and red clover. Cows, he knew, loved clover, it was good for making milk.

Fall was finally here.

The taxi drove up to an elegant farmhouse, two-storey in height, Georgian in style, rather grand and set back from the road, down an avenue of tall poplar trees leading up to the front door that had a small porch overhang. He walked up the gravel path to the front door and knocked.

The door flew open

"Come in, come in. Dora has just put the kettle on." Clancy could hear the clatter of dishes far off in the kitchen.

He entered a long hall, not as grand as the Manor House, but still impressive, with oil paintings and green flush carpet. He was shown to the parlour where Hugh asked him to make himself comfortable while Dora got the tea ready and the delicacies out. It was a pleasant room, the walls covered with rose coloured primrose wallpaper. Big comfortable chairs and a sofa filled the room. A thick Persian rug lay on the floor, a few family portraits hung on the wall. "My late father," said Hugh, pointing to one of an old gentleman sitting with his hunting dog. "This one," he indicated another, "is a family portrait of my parents and us as children." A plate ledge held copper plates depicting scenes of country life, hunters, horses and dogs.

"To whom do we owe the pleasure of your company?" asked Hugh, shaking his hand.

"It's nice to be here. The Gardai want my help. I don't know how I can help them much, but I said I'll do what I can. It's about Sister Gertrude's accident. They're now calling it murder."

"Are they now? That's interesting."

"Yes," said Clancy, "but there are no witnesses. That's the trouble."

"Terrible. terrible news about Sister Gertrude. Do they know how it happened? Someone may have thought she was an animal. It's hunting season. The Gardai could be wrong."

"Do you own a gun?" asked Clancy as casually as possible.

"Yes, but I haven't been out yet. I've got other things to do that are more pressing on my time."

"Do you know of any hunters who live around here?"

"There are lots of farmers who hunt. I can't point to anyone in particular. When the foxes attack the hen house, they get busy, or they kill rats in the barn when they get too big for the cats to kill."

Dora, a sturdy, big boned woman, with generous hips and a pleasant smile, entered the room, exclaiming, "Now gentlemen, let's relax and talk about pleasanter things than Sister Gertrude, a very unpleasant woman in my view." She placed several lace doilies on a small table, then three china plates beside which she added sterling silver forks and spoons, along with three serviettes. She picked up a Royal Doulton teapot. "How would you like your tea, Clancy? Cream and sugar? Fine." She passed the cup and saucer over to him. "And here's a nice piece of chocolate cake that I baked yesterday."

"Thank you," said Clancy, thinking his waistline was going to be much expanded.

"One last question before we leave the topic. Did you see

anyone on the back or front roads that afternoon?"

"After I was coming back from the pub, I did see a small red Volkswagen, go along the back road mid afternoon or thereabouts. Not many people use the back road to our properties, there are no homes on it and no reason to use it. Volkswagen is one of the most popular cars sold in Ireland. You might have a hard time tracking the owner down if you don't have a license number."

"That's interesting," said Clancy, "obviously you'd have left the pub by that time."

"Yes, I had to get back to do chores."

"Do you have any idea who it was?"

"No," he shook his head.

"I'll make a note of that. The coffee and the cake were delicious."

They chatted for awhile about Canada, the weather, his trip into Cork, before Clancy said he should get going.

"Help yourself to another piece of cake before you go," suggested Dora.

"If I do, I'll be as plump as a Christmas Turkey," said Clancy, patting his abdomen. "It was delicious, soft and moist, just the way I like it. My eyes say 'yes', but my stomach says 'no'. Well, got to get back, and thanks for your help."

"It was good to see you and do come again. Sorry that Edward and Quincy weren't here to see you. They've been helping the Squire. Things seemed to be working out."

Clancy asked if he could call a cab. He could squeeze in one more interview before his big date tonight with Tricia.

***

Another person on his list of suspects to call on was farmer Jim Muir. He was in the pub that afternoon and may have heard Sister Gertrude announce her plans.

The Muir's farm was next to Squire Murphy's. Dry stone walls separated the fields, brambles and thorns grew by the roadside. Adding a bit of colour, yellow buttercups flourished in the ditches. At least sheep weren't blocking traffic on the road and the taxi made good time.

There was smoke coming out of the thatched cottage chimney when they pulled up. A good sign. Someone was home.

He had the driver drive up the laneway, so he wouldn't get his feet muddy. Then he dispatched the driver, before he knocked on the green painted wooden front door and heard a 'Hello, who's there?' and the heavy footsteps of Jim Muir coming down the hall.

"Well, hello. Come in. Come in. I'm just going to have a cup of coffee. Will you join me?" asked Jim.

"Sounds good to me," said Clancy following him along a narrow hall with linoleum floor covering and beige walls, from the back of the house to the kitchen. There were red curtains at the large windows. A large pine table sat in the centre of the room, surrounded by cane back chairs. A cactus plant sat on the window ledge. It looked cozy and cheerful.

"Have a seat," said Jim. "Cream and sugar?"

"Thanks."

"You must have heard the village gossip that my wife took off with another man from the village. I guess she got tired of my coming in from the fields and complaining and I got tired of her nagging. We reached a stalemate. Now I've had to manage on my own, but lately Lucy has come to stay and things have been a lot better. She's good company. So, what brings you to this neck of the woods?"

"Well, we're neighbours, and I thought I'd drop by. The Gardai have asked for my help in solving the murder of Sister Gertrude. So, I'm here to ask what you were doing the afternoon that she got shot."

"Helping the Gardai are you? That sounds impressive. Well, see if this helps. Early in the afternoon I was putting away a few at The Crossroads. Then I returned home and went to get wood for a fire, because of my arthritis. I bumped into Quincy on the way and we both went to the woodlot together and then I came home again." That alibi eliminates Jim Muir, thought Clancy.

"Did you see anyone other than Quincy?"

"No, I saw no one."

"Did you see anyone leave the pub when you did?"

"I saw a red Volkswagen pull away from the pub's parking lot just behind me."

"Did you see who was in it?" There's that red Volkswagen again," thought Clancy. Is it just a coincidence that it was on the back road about the time Sister Gertrude was murdered?

"No, I wasn't really looking."

"Well, it's some help," said Clancy. They chatted for a bit, then Clancy thanked Jim Muir for the coffee and strolled back to the Manor House."

***

In his bedroom, Clancy stood in front of the mirror. He'd just had a shower, washed his hair and liberally applied aftershave. He sniffed, he smelled like a pharmacy but that would dissipate. He was ready for the big date. He was nervous. He looked in the mirror. Would he be able to carry it off, a middle-aged man, on a date with a pretty young Colleen? She must fancy him, or she wouldn't be hanging about. He would have to be gentle, take his time, pace himself. Steady at the wheel he told himself.

He put on his new beige cords and long sleeved, tan shirt, then added a jacket and his cloth cap.

Mansbridge saw him on the stairs as he headed out. "There's a spring in your step and a song in your heart."

He took a taxi over to Tricia's house, the address written down on a piece of paper she'd given him. It was a small, white washed cottage with a thatched roof next to a row of several small cottages opposite the village green.

Tricia was standing outside waiting for him, bending over to pull up a weed in her garden. She dropped the weed and gave him a big hug as soon as he walked up the path.

"Welcome to my home." She opened the front door and took off her suede jacket. Underneath, she wore a lovely, white, lace sleeveless dress, thigh-high, with a deep V neck to show off her generous cleavage. He gave her a little peck on the cheek. How soft her skin was. Her hair smelled of apples.

The cottage ceiling was low, with cross oak beams. The pine furniture, a sofa and two chairs looked comfortable, covered with a flowery chintz. Lace curtains at the window. A nice hooked rug on the floor to gave it a homey feeling. Some wall hangings, a stereo in one corner, and a flat TV hung down from the ceiling completed the decor, simple and cozy. Tricia gestured to the TV, suggesting Clancy might like to watch the football matches. "Soccer is very popular here. I'm not so keen on it, but some guests like to watch. Have a seat, make yourself comfortable. Let me, make fresh coffee in the percolator and we can put on some music to relax by. What's your preference? Jazz? Romantic? Pop?"

"I would say, romantic, something by Frank Sinatra, but that dates me. How about something by a Canadian, Michael Bublé or Leonard Cohen?" said Clancy.

"I've got Leonard Cohen's latest. I'll put that on while I go and make the coffee. We can have it with a shot of Bailey's. It goes well with coffee."

After they'd settled on the couch with their coffee, Tricia asked Clancy about his life in Canada.

"Well I have a dog called Jack, a Jack Russell terrier, that I'm very fond of. My first dog, Mike, died of old age." It was hard to avoid saying that he was a married man with responsibilities, but he let the silence do it for him. Omission wasn't exactly lying. He just was on vacation away from work, from home, from everything.

He snuggled in close to her and gave her a small kiss on the cheek. Tricia blushed. They drank their coffee and then Tricia poured some more liquor, just to keep the chill off.

She gently laid her soft, warm hand on his thigh, which was pressed against her He could feel the heat in him, the bulge in his trousers was rising. All signals were go. Nice and slow he reminded himself. Let her make the first move. Anticipation is everything.

She patted his thigh and smiled at him. He leaned in to kiss those lush red lips of hers.

Just then the phone rang.

"Oh, leave it," said Clancy groaning, "Just when we're in the midst of something important. Return the call later. You have better things to do, Tricia."

"Oh, but I'm on call this weekend, for emergencies. It'll just take a second."

She picked up the phone. "Yes, yes, can't it wait? I am occupied at the moment." She gave Clancy a fond look. "Oh, it can't. I'll be right over." She hung up and turned to Clancy." I have to go. I am really sorry about this, really, I am. I can give you a lift back to the Manor house on my way. Mrs. O'Sullivan is in labour, her water's broke, and the baby is due at any moment."

Clancy stood up saying as graciously he could muster, "How disappointing, how very disappointing." It seemed like the mouse had escaped from the trap, the deer from the hunter, the rabbit from the hawk.

"It can't be helped," said Tricia. "That's my job. Never mind, there's always another day, another time. That's life."

"Yeah," said Clancy, "that's life." Not too pleased at all at the outcome, but tomorrow was another day.

***

The next morning ping, ping went his phone. Clancy rolled over in bed and, opening one eye, picked it up. He had a throbbing headache. It was not going to be a good day.

"Hello, hello, who is it?" asked Clancy, in a really bad mood. He glanced at his watch. It was nine thirty.

"Agnes, your wife. Who did you think it was? Who were you expecting?"

"Oh, oh, he thought, trouble ahead." "I've got a bit of a hang-over, luv."

"In the pub last night, were you? I phoned late last night and Mansbridge said you weren't in." She sounded suspicious.

"Got in quite late." He hoped that Mansbridge had done a good job of covering up for him.

"So, I can tell. How are things going with the investigation?"

"Things are just crawling along, rather boring but that's the way life is, the same thing, day in, day out." Clancy bit his tongue when he said it. "How about you, luv?"

"Well, grin and bear it. The reason for my call is that your dog is showing antisocial tendencies. It's taken to pissing on the piano legs in the living room. It's going to destroy the wood eventually. It's a very good piano, a Heintzman, as you know. I've sprayed hot pepper on it's legs, but I can't get him to stop. This has all happened since you went to Ireland. The dog misses you and that's why he's doing it. Well what are you going to do about it?"

Clancy paused and let her continue.

"Not only that, but when I'm tending the vegetable garden, a red wing blackbird comes out of nowhere and is making dive bombs at my head. I'm thinking of getting a cat to keep the bird away."

Clancy pictured his broad beamed wife bending over with the beak of the bird aiming at her behind. He suppressed a chuckle. He would try to reason with her. "Agnes, It's not like I'm away for a month. It is just another week and a few days. "My advice is, don't let the dog into the living room. Keep the living room doors closed. Hang in there, Agnes, until I get back. Don't let the wild life get to you. I 'm not a cat lover, Agnes. You know that. Cats are not my style. No cats. I am allergic to cats. Please don't buy one. Love you." He hung up the phone. He couldn't believe it, an expensive phone call all the way from Canada about a dog pissing on the piano legs and a bird dive bombing in the garden. A flood or a fire would have justified the call. "Get a life, Agnes," he thought.

Chapter 18

After breakfast, Clancy walked out to the apple orchard and looked around on the ground for a couple of good apples that had fallen off the trees, ones that had no worm holes in them and weren't badly bruised. He found two and put them into his jacket pocket. He walked over to the fence where Nellie, a lovely chestnut mare, had come over to see him and was nosing the wooden barrier. He held out an apple on his flat palm. Nellie opened her mouth and chomped down on it. Clancy rubbed her mane. She whinnied. A beautiful horse, thought Clancy, nice and gentle. He wished that he could own a horse, but he didn't have deep pockets. Oh, he was loving the life here, but he must get back to sleuthing.

On the afternoon that Sister Gertrude was murdered, who were the people around at that time who might have seen her go down the road, cross the field and into the woodlot? There were several possibilities. Inside the house there was Mansbridge and the housekeeper, long time, loyal servants and hardly suspects. Outdoors, Edward was working in the barn and so was Quincy. They were possibilities. So, he decided to go in pursuit of Edward.

"Ah, the young and restless," said Clancy spying Edward loping around the corner of the barn in his wellington boots.

"There's too much work to be done to be young and restless." he replied. "There are two farms now to manage, not just one, Dad's and the Squire's, now that Seamus is gone. I can't do everything, and everyone thinks I can. Everyone has put everything on my shoulders." He kicked a small rock out of his path with the toe of his boot.

"I thought Quincy was helping you."

Edward grimaced, "Usually, Quincy does what Quincy wants to do."

"Oh, I thought you were on good terms."

"We are, we are," he snarled.

"Busy last Saturday afternoon?"

"I was cleaning out the stables, getting straw for the horses, that sort of thing."

"Did you have help from Quincy?"

"Yes, he was helping me out. Then he got the idea to go and shoot grouse. It was the opening of hunting season. I was left on my own for a time, as usual."

"Is Quincy very good with a gun?"

"Yes, he practices. Nails tin cans to the fence and aims at them, that sort of thing. Mostly he shoots rabbits and rats."

"Seen anyone, Saturday, down near the woodlot?"

"Can't say I did. Too busy to notice."

"So, you two were apart for the latter part of the afternoon.

"You could say that." said Edward looking down at his boots.

Clancy smiled, "But you still had time for a pint."

"Yes, I was in the pub that afternoon. So was everybody else including Quincy. It was the weekend, time to relax."

"Did you hear Sister Gertrude in the pub announce that she was going down to the woodlot, to find the Mass Stone?"

"I didn't hear her. So many people were talking. It was hard to hear. What's it to you?"

"She had a fairly loud voice."

"Well I didn't hear her. Later Quincy showed up and joined me for a pint of beer and then we went back to the manor. I needed his help in rounding up the cows. Say, aren't you asking a lot of questions?"

"The Gardai want my help. They've asked me to find out if there might have been any witnesses."

"I can't help." He kicked at another stone. "Maybe Quincy can tell you something." He headed into the barn.

There's is a lot of resentment in that young, unhappy man, thought Clancy. He headed back across the field to the Manor house and rang the side bell to get in. No one came. He rang it again. No one answered. I guess Mansbridge is not available or he would have come to the door. He was locked out. Clancy decided to go back down to the barn and ask Edward, on the off chance, if he had a key.

Edward took out a chain from his pocket and fingered the circular ring. "Yes, I have. Here it is. After you let yourself in, you can leave the key on the kitchen counter. I'll be up there for tea."

"Edward has a key to the house, now that's interesting," thought Clancy. If Edward's key opened the back door to the manor house, how many more keys were out there? He would ask Mansbridge later. He should know. He found Mansbridge, in the library straightening out the bookshelves. He probably hadn't heard him knocking on the back door.

Mansbridge looked up when he saw Clancy.

"How can I help you?"

"I'm curious, Mansbridge, how many keys are there to the back door?"

"The housekeeper has one. I have one, the Squire has one and Edward, who is helping out on the farm. There are only four keys. Why do you ask?"

"Just curious. Where are the keys hung?"

"I keep mine, and the housekeeper keeps hers on a chain just inside the back door. Edward, you will have to ask him."

"Was there any break and enter, do you think, when the Squire fell on the stairs? Did anyone get into the house?"

"Not to my knowledge. The doors are locked and the house is secured. It's funny you should ask that. I noticed some scratch marks on the spindles of the banister near where he fell. But I thought nothing of it."

"Any alarm system?"

"There is. The alarm pad is set beside the back door with numbers to punch in. Everyone knows the numbers. It's no secret. We all know them."

"So, as far as you know, no one got hold of the keys and made a duplicate."

"Yes, I'm pretty sure of that. They've never gone missing."

Clancy decided to walk back to the barn where he found Edward working away cleaning out the stalls.

"Edward, thanks for letting me borrow your keys. I was going to ask you, where do you keep your keys? They're pretty heavy to keep in your pocket."

"I hang them on the barn wall, on that hook over there, when I don't need to use them. Anything else? I've got work to do. I'm not on vacation like you," He turned his back on Clancy to continue shoveling the straw and manure out of the stall.

***

One little mystery was solved, a bunch of keys to the Manor house were left on a nail in the barn where anyone could take them, make a copy and get into the house during the night. The Squire had no hired hands except his two nephews. Edward seemed very trustworthy, but his brother?

He heard the noise of a goat smashing its horns against the wooden wall. "Baaaaa. Baaaaa." It went on and on. He wished he had an apple for the goat to shut it up.

Clancy decided to have a look around. First, he checked out the pig pen, then the stalls where the cows were kept for milking after they'd been brought in from the fields at night. He kept looking until he finally found Quincy

"Oh, a word, Quincy." Quincy looked up, surprised to see him. His overalls were covered in straw.

He stopped shoveling up the muck and manure and then leaned his shovel carefully against the barn wall.

He scowled and looked down at his feet. "Yeah, what brings you here? I heard from my brother that you've been going around asking a lot of questions about that old bitch that got shot to death by accident."

"By accident? The Gardai don't think so. They don't think it was a hunter who shot her by mistake and have asked me to make inquiries. You were in the pub and then you went to the woodlot that afternoon. Did you see anyone there?"

"Not a soul. Just my mate, the neighbouring farmer, Jim Muir. We went there to get firewood. I helped him get it. Afterwards we split. I did a little shooting on my own.

"Exactly where? Anywhere near the Mass Rock?"

"Don't know what that is. When we split after Jim collected the wood for his fireplace, I came back and did some target practice. Just shooting here and there, no place in particular. In the woodlot and around."

"And you didn't see anyone? Coming or going in the woodlot?"

"Not that I recall. Wasn't really looking," Quincy glanced sullenly at Clancy.

"Quincy, I want to bring up something that has happened while I've been staying here. During the night someone has been prowling around the ground floor of the Manor House. There have been no break-ins. The locks weren't picked, so the person must have had a key. It was an inside job. My next question is, where did they get the key? Apparently, one set was hung in the barn, available to anyone. Who worked in the barn? You and Edward."

"What are you getting at?" Quincy snarled.

"Supposing someone wanted to give the Squire a scare and took the keys and got into the Manor house at night while everyone was sleeping."

"Well, don't ask me, I know nothing about it. I have a lot of chores to do and all this talk is keeping me from doing them."

"Do you think Edward would do something like that? Edward comes across as being a very responsible person." Clancy watched his face for a reaction. There was none.

"By the way, Quincy, what do you like to shoot at for target practice?"

"Raccoons. Rabbits. Squirrels are great fun. Hedgehogs, porcupines, anything that moves or catches my fancy. I shot the family cat by mistake. It was an old cat, I put it out of its misery. Quick and painless. Why do you ask?"

"Just curious. How do you like working here?"

"I have no choice. There are no other jobs available. I need the cash. Got a girl and need money to pay for dates. No money, no honey. I don't know how long the Squire will be off."

"Sabrina seems a nice catch," said Clancy. "I hope you're treating her well."

"What business is it of yours? How do you know?" demanded Quincy giving him a hard stare.

"A little bird told me."

"Well, keep your nose out of my affairs. I don't like people meddling in my affairs. It could be dangerous," he snarled.

"If you see anything, let me know. I'm staying on to help the Gardai." A real piece of work, thought Clancy. Intuition tells me that it was Quincy who broke into the house. Why? He was low man on the totem pole and, by killing the Squire on the stairs, he would come into some inheritance.

On his way out of the barn, Clancy stooped to wipe some muck off his shoe. A pitchfork whizzed by above his head and rammed itself into the wooden barn wall. He whirled around, but no one was there, just stacks of hay and an empty room.

He ran back through the other areas of the barn but could find no one.

Too close for comfort, just missed me by a few centimetres, he thought. Someone had tried to scare him. No, it was worse than that. Someone had tried to kill him.

He went over to the wall to examine the pitchfork, which was deeply embedded in the wood.

He pulled out his cell phone and punched in the numbers for the Gardai and asked for Sergeant Finney.

"Finney speaking."

"Clancy here. I just had an awful scare. Someone tried to kill me. A pitchfork was thrown at my head, narrowly missing me."

"Do you have any idea who did it?"

"No, when I looked around the person who had thrown it had vanished. But Quincy Murphy verbally threatened me, in a conversation that I had with him, about ten minutes prior to the incident."

"I'll come right over and take a look."

Ten minutes later, Finney showed up and parked his car outside the barn. Clancy was waiting for him at the door. He took him inside and showed him the pitchfork embedded in the wooden wall. "It just missed my head by centimeters."

"I can take it to the lab for fingerprints," said Finney," but I imagine that they have all been wiped off. This is disturbing news, Clancy. You'll have to watch your back from here on in. I advise staying away from the barn and the woodlot just in case.

"It's difficult for us because you didn't actually see anyone do it. We can't lay a criminal charge without some kind of evidence, without a witness. What I can do is take Quincy in for questioning, down at the office. I'll try to give him a bit of a scare, I'll inform him that we believe he threw the pitchfork, then tell him that, from here on in, he'd better not do anything unusual as we'll be watching him"

"Yes, that's a good idea. I realize that you can't lay a formal charge, but I can lay a formal complaint in case he plans anything similar in the foreseeable future. In my experience, there's never just one criminal act."

"That's a good idea. Keep in touch, Clancy, and be careful. Be very careful."

"Will do."

Clancy walked slowly back to the Manor House and let himself in the side door. He looked down at his hands which were shaking and put them in his pocket. He needed a drink to settle his nerves, and put his feet up, to get his bearing on things and to put that attempt on his life out of his mind.

The Squire, who was sitting in the library reading his newspaper looked up. "You look as white as a ghost. What happened?"

Clancy told him about the incident in the barn.

"This is appalling news," said the Squire. "Have you any idea of who might have done it?"

"Nothing that can be proven at this point in time. I could name somebody, but I would hate to be wrong."

"I see," said the Squire. "I'll ring Mansbridge for a drink. How about a Bloody Mary?"

"That would be great. My nerves are shot."

"Mine would be too," said the Squire, sympathetically shaking his head.

Clancy sat quietly sipping his drink and marveling at the close call he'd had. After a while he felt better. There was still time before dinner to drop into the pub, so Clancy headed down the road. Inside, he spied Jim Muir having a pint and waved him over.

"Jim, how's the world treating you?"

"It's as good as it gets."

"Nice afternoon coffee I had at your cottage the other day."

"Well, do come again, you know we're just down the road."

"Tell me, Jim, who were you drinking with the afternoon of the murder? Can you remember?"

"Well, I was chatting with Lucy at the bar a good deal of the time. She was pouring pints with Kathleen. Then I went over and joined a group of men. I can't recall all their names off hand."

"Was this before Sister Gertrude left or after?"

"It was after. Mid-afternoon. Then I broke off and headed back to the farm.

"No idea who they were."

"No, we were chatting about the weather and the problems that come with too much rain, the run off of the soil." He put his empty glass down. "No time for another, got to get the cows in and get some milking done. See you." He headed out the door.

Clancy walked over to two tall men in denim overalls and Wellington boots, nursing pints. They both looked like they were in their early forties. He introduced himself. Maybe they had something to tell him.

"Hi, I'm Clancy, over here for a vacation. Sorry, I don't know your names." He extended his hand.

"I'm Liam, said the taller one with the black moustache and black, bushy eyebrows. His thumb was black and blue, from a hammer blow? His fingers gripping the beer glass were huge. Strong as an ox, thought Clancy. "This," he said, pointing to the man next to him, "is Gerry." Gerry just nodded, "Pleased to meet you."

"Hunting season is open. Get in a little hunting?" asked Clancy.

"Not yet, it's a little early," said Liam. Gerry just shook his head.

"Were you in the pub last Saturday afternoon?"

"Might have been. Like to drop in for a pint, talk to the other farmers. Why?"

"Did you see a nun in here, a middle-aged nun, that afternoon?".

"Not to my knowledge. What did she look like?

"White hair. She was wearing a grey suit, white shirt with a long silver cross dangling from her neck."

"Nah, we just like talking to the young Colleens, like Lucy and Katherine, behind the bar. Old birds don't interest us. We like them young and frisky. Why do you ask?"

"She got her head blown off in the woodlot later that afternoon, after she'd been here."

"Did she now? I do remember hearing something about a nun getting bumped off. Very unusual. I was brought up a Catholic but have strayed from the path. Lapsed, so to speak. So is Gerry here. Here's to our health." He took another sip of his drink.

Clancy drifted back to his stool at the bar thinking, the killer must have had some connection with her, a relationship. Who noticed her? Who listened to her? That was the catch. Not all the farmers are practicing Catholics and go to mass, some have lapsed. Sister Gertrude is not a familiar figure to everyone. He looked down at his glass which was half empty.

"Hello." A voice at his elbow jarred him out of his reverie. A labourer with paint splashes on his overalls was standing next to him. "Hello, I overheard you ask about that nun, a middle-aged woman in a grey suit with a large silver cross. I remember seeing her that afternoon. She was quite excited about a Mass Rock. Hyper, shouting almost. Nuns can get so excited about nothing."

"Did you see anyone leave when she did?"

"Yes, several people headed for the door after she left.

"Did you notice anyone in particular?"

"Can't say I did. Sorry I can't be more helpful."

"Thanks, anyhow."

Clancy spied a familiar figure at the bar, Doc Flannery, who had just come in. "How's it going, Doc? Your health. that is?"

"Some days are good. Some days are not so good. But a pint of Guinness helps the waterworks, sluices the pipes, keeps the flow going. And you?"

"Well apart from a hernia operation, things are going

smoothly. Had it done at the Shouldice Clinic in Toronto. In one day and out the next."

"Well, I wish things were that simple for me. Old age is supposed to kill you off, but I think, by the way things are going, it will be my prostate. The test results, the PSAs are high, not good. They think the cancer cells have metastasized, gone loose into other organs of my body, even after surgery and radiation when they thought they'd gotten every single cell. It just takes one cell to get loose. So, I want to drink up and be merry while I still can. Here's to your health. How's the investigation going? Are you making any headway?"

"Early stages still. Not much to go on. No witnesses. But it must be somebody from the pub, no one else would know that she was in the woodlot. What are your thoughts on the matter?"

"I haven't any. I'm in the dark as much as you are, although I think the Gardai have got it wrong. I think she was shot mistakenly by a hunter. Some hunter did us a favour."

"In the pub that day, did you see anyone slip out early? Did you see anyone drinking by themselves?"

"Can't say I did. I was chatting with Hugh Murphy and Edward. We were talking among ourselves and I didn't notice anything. Shortly after Sister Gertrude left, Hugh left and so did Edward. to go back to work. I stayed on.

"Whom did you talk to?"

"Can't remember. I'd had several pints by that time."

"So, you were alone?"

"Yes, I can't vouch for my drinking companions. Local farmers. I don't recall their names."

"I see. Keep your eyes and ears open for me, will you?" asked Clancy.

"Sure thing." Doc Flannery lifted his glass to his lips. "But I don't know how good my eyesight is. Just kidding."

Chapter 19

Sitting in his office study, below a large silver cross on the wall with the prostrate figure of Christ nailed to it, Father Flynn rubbed his temples trying to gain some insight into Sister Gertrude's murder. Sister Gertrude had been murdered in a woodlot by an unknown person with a shotgun. Would the killer come looking for him? Would he be next? He felt a headache coming on.

He got up and walked back and forth across the room, scratching his head. Then he went over to his desk and opened the bottom drawer and reached in. He took out a bottle of whisky and took a healthy slug, then replaced it in the drawer and shut it. Feeling better about things, he thought about it hard. Sister Gertrude had enemies. Who were his enemies? It would be hard to name one.

Unlike Sister Gertrude, he got along quite well with his parishioners, at least he thought he did. He was careful not to judge, *lest yea be judged. God was the ultimate judge.* He liked to leave things open ended and ambiguous, with no finger-pointing. To those who heard them, his homilies were designed to allow his parishioners to engage in self reflection.

Above all, he wanted to be loved.

Would that mean, he wondered, that instead of being the good shepherd guiding his people, he was one of the flock, a sheep? Had he followed instead of led? Was the local pub where he drank with the locals really his church?

As for confession, not many came to confession anymore. He could sit in that dark, cramped, sweaty confession booth waiting for ever. Few came, only the elderly and the very young. Today, so many of his parishioners did not recognize the word 'sin'. The young men who came confessed that they masturbated and couldn't stop. Would they go blind? Not likely. There are greater sins than masturbation.

He thought about one of the ten commandments, *'Do not commit adultery'*. That was a tough one, and very hard to keep in these parts. He had heard rumours, gossip, that spread like wildfire throughout the community about people who strayed from their marriage vows and became engaged in extra-marital affairs. To that thought, he countered with, *'Let him without sin cast the first stone.'*

He wondered if he'd taken the wrong road. In his youth, he felt he was called by God to be a priest. His mother had wanted him to be a priest. It was just something understood in his family, that he was the chosen one. But, as he got older, he no longer felt the same keenness. He lacked the dedication and fervor of his youth. He lacked the passion for the position. Now, he went where he was sent, to parishes that held no interest for him. He felt he wasn't making a difference.

As a young priest, just after he had been ordained, he had fire in his belly when he was posted to Harlem, New York, to work with African Americans, establishing soup kitchens, clinics, daycare and visiting centres. There was a real need for him there. He'd felt wanted. He'd felt needed. The work was tiring, but at the end of the day he was fulfilled. Now, at forty, he was in this quiet backwater of Cork County, surrounded by villages and farmland with only the elderly for solace. The church in Ireland was dying. In spirit he was dying with it.

He was stuck alone in a parish manse with an old house-keeper for company. No children, no wife, and no dependents. If he had to confess to anything, it would be the lust in his heart that would not go away. He was falling apart and could do nothing to stop it.

He needed more help, another nun to go around the parish visiting the sick and the elderly to replace Sister Gertrude. He couldn't do the work all by himself. They wouldn't send one right away, it would take time. The Bishop would send the ugliest middle-aged nun he could find, having the sort of face that no man would look at twice. He checked himself at his unkind thoughts.

His reverie was interrupted by a knock at the door.

"Come in, come in," he said. "Are you here for confession? Love the sinner but hate the sin."

132

Clancy glanced around the room, at its monastic bareness. Father Flynn's black cassock hanging on a hanger in a closet with no door, an old battered desk, on which sat his black missal and an empty coffee mug, a frayed rug on the floor and the silver cross behind him on the wall. A small table held his black landline telephone and a lap top, the only extravagant gesture in the room. The room looked bleak and barren.

Clancy thought that Father Flynn was a little too merry for this hour of the morning.

"No, unfortunately not. I came on another matter." Clancy hadn't been to confession in years and he wasn't going to start now. "The Gardai, as I've mentioned, have asked for my help in finding out who killed Sister Gertrude."

"I would be glad to help, but I don't see what I can offer. Pull up a chair. Make yourself comfortable."

"The only people who knew Sister Gertrude was going into the woodlot to find the Mass Rock were the customers at The Crossroads. I understand you were there. Do you recall who you were talking to?

"It's hard to recall. I was talking to one person and then another, drifting around the room."

"Can you recall their names?"

Father Flynn paused, "Hugh Murphy, then his sons, Quincy and Edward, Doc Flannery, some farmers. I don't recall their names off hand."

"My most important question is, did you see anyone leave shortly after Sister Gertrude left?"

"I wasn't watching the door, nor did I see anyone slip away. I had had several pints by then and was feeling rather mellow, as one might say. Who came and who went, I have no idea."

"Do you know of anyone who had it in for Sister Gertrude? Who would hate her enough to kill her?"

Father Flynn shook his head. "Unfortunately, Sister Gertrude had a knack for stirring up things, acerbating things, pouring acid on personal wounds. I shouldn't speak ill of the dead," he sighed. "I'm afraid that I can't be much help to you."

Clancy thanked him and got up to leave.

"Can I give you a ride? I have to visit a sick old lady and it'll be no trouble at all."

"Thanks, I accept your kind offer."

133

Chapter 20

Clancy was doing some hard thinking, but he couldn't yet see a light at the end of the tunnel, the woods for the trees. He was running out of time. Soon he would have to return to Mariposa and he hadn't much to show for his sleuthing.

He decided to look up Doc Flannery again, on his own turf, using the excuse that he wanted advice on the arthritis in his feet which had begun to bother him with all that rain they had lately. From Mansbridge he got Doc Flannery's surgery hours, which were mostly in the morning, and after breakfast he had him call a cab for the ride to the small village nearby where Doc Flannery lived.

It was a small white washed cottage with a thatched roof, white lace curtains covering the front window, a rose garden in front, and with a black sign stuck in the middle that said *Surgery*. A wheelbarrow filled with geraniums was parked near the front door. He walked up the cobblestone path to the door and rang the bell. A middle-aged woman in a white smock opened the door. His housekeeper?

"Clancy Murphy?" she said. "Doc Flannery will see you shortly. Sit down in the hall for a few minutes and make yourself comfortable."

Clancy looked at the walls, hung with diplomas and certificates. Then he picked up a magazine, *Country Life,* flipping through the pages. A tangerine coloured cat wandered in and rubbed itself against his legs. meowing loudly. Probably covered in fleas, thought Clancy. "Shoo, scat, get lost."

"Well, hello. What brings you here?" Doc Flannery was standing in the doorway with his stethoscope around his neck.

"Arthritis in my feet. It's very painful."

"Come in, come."

Clancy followed Doc Flannery into the surgery. He glanced around at the large mahogany desk and black leather chair, thick medical books lining the shelves on the wall. In a corner the glass medicine cabinet with its pills and douches, the leather couch placed next to the desk, the weighing scale and height measuring stick, the enamel sterilizer half hidden behind a white curtain, all very clean, neat and organized.

"How are things?" asked Clancy. "Haven't see you at the Manor house lately."

"I have had my spells, sometimes not feeling so well. Now, getting back to you. Arthritis is a bit tricky, an auto immune disease. It comes and goes without any reason. Take off your socks and shoes. Let me see your feet."

Clancy hoped they didn't smell. He'd taken a hot shower that morning in preparation for his visit and put on fresh clean socks.

"Put your right foot up on the stool."

Clancy did as he was told.

Doc Flannery quickly washed his hands and then bent down to examine Clancy's fat toes, pulling them slowly apart as he did so.

"Nice little porkies," he commented. "At least they're dry, and I see no cracks in the skin between the toes. No sign of athlete's foot or any other fungus at the moment. Make sure your feet are powdered with talcum powder before you put your socks on each day. There's swelling at the joints. That's your arthritis. If it was in your hands, your fingers would be bent a little.

"My advice is to wear wool socks. Try to keep your feet warm. Dry them well after a shower. My best suggestion is to take high doses of fish oil or omega three. Glucosamine with chronditin is not a bad idea. I see no corns or bunions or evidence of plantar fasciitis, common for someone who spends a lot of time on his feet."

"Thanks for the advice. Will do." Clancy pulled his socks back on again. To change the subject he asked, "Now how is it going with you, Doc? Your health that is?"

"Some days are good. Some days, not so good. Statistically over 70 percent of men get prostate cancer at seventy. This increases to 80 percent at 80. I'm seventy-seven. By the way how's the investigation going? Are you making any headway?"

That was just the subject that Clancy wanted to bring up.

"Early stages still. Not much to go on. No witnesses. But it must be somebody from the pub, otherwise no one else would know that she was in the woodlot. What are your thoughts on the matter?" He stared hard at Doc Flannery.

"I haven't any. I am in the dark as much as you are. I think the Gardai have got it wrong. I think she was shot mistakenly by a hunter."

"The last time we met I asked you did you see anyone slip out early? Did you see anyone drinking by themselves? Have you remembered anything to change your mind? Can you recall anything different than what you last told me?"

"Can't say I do. I was chatting with Father Flynn, Hugh Murray, Quincy and Edmund. We were talking among ourselves and I didn't notice anything. Shortly after Gertrude left, Hugh left and so did Edmund to go back to work. I stayed on."

"Who did you talk to?"

"Can't remember. I had had several pints by that time."

"So, you were alone?"

"I can't vouch for my drinking companions. Local farmers and I don't recall their names."

"I see. I'd hope you'd remembered something. Keep your eyes and ears open for me, will you? I will need all the help I can get," said Clancy. Will someone kindly call a cab for me. I'm going back to the Manor House."

"Will do. If you have any other medical problems be sure to come and see me."

"Will do."

Chapter 21

It was a sunny day, with no rain sight. Tricia parked her car carefully in a parking space in the pub's parking lot which was rather full. She got out and headed for the pub's front door in search of Clancy, knowing that he would probably be there. Indeed, he was sitting by the fire nursing a pint.

"Oh, Clancy, I am so glad I found you. I'm so sorry about the other night and being called away. It was a medical emergency and I was on call. I want to make it up to you, I really do." She thrust her eager face up into his. "Will you be able to drop by this evening?" She reached for his hand and gave it a squeeze.

"That would be nice." Privately, Clancy thought that with Tricia he was like a car on the highway of life, full speed ahead then the brakes were suddenly applied, full speed ahead then the brakes bringing the car to a full stop. This speeding and stopping was giving him heartburn. Was he going to get lucky or was he not?

"I'll take the phone off the hook, just the two of us relaxing to some nice music over drinks. No interruptions this time."

"I'll drink to that," said Clancy. "Sit down and I'll buy you a pint. Tell me how you're doing."

"Sounds good to me," said Tricia, taking a chair beside him. "I can drink a pint with you and then I have to be off. It was an interesting case that I had to treat this morning. We get the odd one. A young farmer had been vacationing in Greece and met up with an English girl. They took to dancing all night. He got back home about a week ago. All things were fine until he noticed a red ulcer on his genitals and then one in his mouth. I told him that it might be syphilis and only a blood test would confirm it. If caught early syphilis is easily treated with one shot of penicillin. Sad to say, though, VD is on the rise among the young. Well, Clancy, I am still a working girl. I have to go. See you tonight."

***

After supper, Clancy took a shower and put on his best clothes and a pair of clean jockey shorts.

He told Mansbridge where he was going, would be back late and asked him to call a cab.

The taxi took him to Tricia's cottage in the village but first he stopped at a wayside kiosk to buy a bouquet of red roses.

The porch light was on. He knocked on the door.

"Come in, come in," shouted Tricia." I'm just slipping into something comfortable." She came out of a back room wearing a voluminous silk negligee, tied at the neck with pink ribbons.

"Oh, you look smashing," said Clancy, his spirits rising.

"I just wear this on special occasions," said Tricia. "Come and sit down on the couch. What lovely flowers. Thank you for thinking of me. I'll go and put them in a nice vase with water so that they won't wilt.

"What will you have to drink, Clancy? Gin and Tonic, or Rum and Coke?"

"Gin and Tonic sounds good."

Tricia went over to the drink cart and poured the drink and handed it to him. "Sorry, there's no lemon. I'll get some ice from the freezer. Sit back and enjoy."

Clancy felt a little nervous. Was he going to get lucky tonight? All signs said 'yes'.

Tricia sat down and snuggled up to him. "Are you ticklish? Let me see if you're ticklish?" She began digging her long nails into his side making him laugh.

"I'm very sensitive, Tricia. Don't torture me like that. That is cruelty." How could he get serious if she kept tickling him? "Please stop."

She finally did. "I should tell you about my day. I had to visit Paddy Johnson again. He lives in the next village. I went to his home. His dog greeted me at the door with several loud farts," Tricia laughed, "Paddy Johnson didn't hear me coming along the hall. He was sitting naked in a chair in his bedroom, with his pajamas fallen down around his ankles, playing with himself. I felt so embarrassed for him. I've seen it all, being a nurse. It's nothing new to me."

"What did you do?"

"I backed out of the room for, a few minutes, to let him cover himself up, and pull up his pajamas, etc. When I walked back in, I pretended that I hadn't seen anything. I acted as if nothing had happened.

"Oh, Clancy, I have seen it all. I have seen HIV sores, bleeding ulcers, white crabs, grayish fungal infections all in and around a man's genitals. You name it, I have seen it. Nothing fazes me."

Clancy choked on his drink. What doe she expect to find on me? Does she think my dick is bent and is trying to save me from embarrassment? Does she expect to find a dent in my dick? I hope this is not turning out to be a clinical exercise and that I am under the microscope? It is hard to get romantic under clinical eyes in a lab. Maybe that's her nature to be outspoken and frank. This is how she acts naturally. Finding a sore on a dick is all in a day's work.

"Let's change the subject. Tricia, you have the loveliest lips. So kissable."

Tricia laughed. "Then you must do something."

Clancy leaned in for a long, hard smooch. But somehow his ardour wasn't the same. The spell had been broken. The magic of the moment had flown. His energy had evaporated. He took another long sip of his drink. He thought of that childish verse, lips that touch liquor will never touch mine.

Tricia noticed that he was acting a bit off. She reached down and stroked his thigh. "Oh, Clancy, was I too clinical about my work? Let's get into the mood again." She snuggled closer to him. He smelled her perfume, but it wasn't enough to get his mojo up and at it.

"You're a good nurse, Tricia, dedicated to your work, which is something to be proud of. It's just me, not you."

They sipped their drinks in silence. Clancy finally said," it was nice to come over. I've had a wonderful stay in Ireland, everyone has been so hospitable. I'll be leaving soon but have lots of wonderful memories. Would you call a taxi for me to go back to the Manor house? No hard feelings, luv, I'm just not up to it."

"Oh, I'm sorry about that. Sorry you have to go. I had hoped that you would stay overnight. But if you insist."

Soon the taxi was there. He gave her a peck on the cheek, thanked her again and said goodbye as graciously as he could muster, then got into the cab and headed back to the Squire's feeling rather deflated about the outcome of the evening.

***

When Mansbridge opened the door, and led him into the library, he found the Squire standing in front of the fire waiting up for him. "Your time with us, Clancy, sadly is drawing to a close. You've been such good company, I'll miss you now that I'm back on my feet."

"The feeling is mutual. I appreciated staying here so much."

"Did you come to any conclusion in your investigation?"

"Well yes and no. The trouble is that there's nothing that I can prove. It would be libelous if I named somebody and the police can't make an arrest."

"I see," said the Squire, "that's all you can say?"

"Yes, it's better to err on the side of caution, but I have something to say to you about security around here. I think you should change the locks on the doors and not let Edward hang the keys to the house in the barn. There, they're available to anyone. I'm not casting any aspersions on Edward. Edward seems trustworthy and very responsible."

"And Quincy?"

Clancy grimaced. "How shall I put it? He shows a streak of cruelty to the animals that he shoots which is not a good sign. He shows signs of violence. Often people who mistreat and kill animals go on to commit even more violent acts against people."

"Yes, I heard that he shot the family cat. He claimed, by mistake."

"I'm not so sure," said Clancy slowly. "A word to the wise. I wouldn't let Quincy have access to your house. That's my advice for what it's worth. I wouldn't turn my back on him. I was in the barn yesterday. After talking to Quincy. I bent down to clean my shoes off, a pitchfork came flying through the air, narrowly missing my head. When I looked around, no one was there. I could have been badly injured. There are no witnesses, but I strongly believe that it was Quincy who threw it. There's no doubt in my mind. I've informed the Gardai to keep an eye on him. They've questioned him, but no charges have yet been laid. I would hazard a guess that Quincy was behind the wire strung across the bottom of the stairs which made you fall. "

"You found a wire strung across the stairs?"

"Yes, your fall was not an accident. When I went back to

142

examine the stairs, I found the broken wire still attached to a nail. I'm pretty sure Quincy had used the keys that were hung on the barn wall to enter the house during the night. There was no break and enter, so it had to be an internal job. Mansbridge and your housekeeper are very loyal staff so that rules them out. That leaves Quincy, who had everything to gain by you falling and killing yourself on the stairs.

"That's alarming news. Are you quite sure?" The squire turned pale and his hands shook. Finally, he spoke. "It's such disappointing news for me. I had such high hopes for my nephew, that he would straighten himself out and become a reliable worker, a decent human being. It will be hard to explain things to his father. Like every father you want the best for your children. I'll make sure the locks are changed immediately and that Quincy has no way of getting in. You've given me much to think about, Clancy. It saddens me greatly. It'll take some getting use to. Thanks for everything."

"I have you to thank for your generous hospitality. I'm sorry that I'm not able to give you better news."

"You did your best and I'm grateful. As for the Mass Rock, thankfully it will not become a tourist attraction, not with the fact that a nun was murdered there, I would have hated to see people tramping over my property to get to it, a tourist site, over my dead body."

Chapter 22

That night, not able to get to sleep, Clancy went over the happenings of the last couple of weeks. For some time, his prime suspect had been Quincy. He had a rifle and was a good shot. He had opportunity that afternoon. He had gone to the woodlot with Jim Muir to collect fire wood. It would have been easy later to retrace his steps, find Sister Gertrude and shoot her. But the problem with Quincy committing the murder is that he didn't appear to have a strong motive. Sure, he disliked her and said so, but that wasn't enough for him to want to kill her. Or was it?

The killer had to be someone with a strong motive, not to have held the common idea that Sister Gertrude was a bitch. It had to be something more than that. It had to be a murder of opportunity, overhearing her conversation, then making the decision to head out to the Mass Rock where she would be found. The rifle must have been kept in the trunk of a car, for the hunting season.

A red Volkswagen had been seen leaving the parking lot at the same time as Jim Muir left the pub, which was also the time Sister Gertrude left. This same car was seen on the back road behind the woodlot by Hugh Murphy. Can we assume that both cars were the same?

Doc Flannery owns a red Volkswagen. Sister Gertrude accused him of carrying out abortion and committing euthanasia. She had complained to the Gardai about him and tried to get him put behind bars.

Clancy's suspicions focused now on Doc Flannery. He was old and in poor health, with not much time to live. He had nothing to lose by murdering her. Another chat with him was in order.

He slept soundly until he woke up around eight. The sun was shining through the window. It was going to be a nice day with no rain.

***

In the dining room Mansbridge greeted him. "I'm sorry that you're leaving us so soon. I'll be sorry to see you go."

"Can't be helped. Have to get back to work."

After another hearty breakfast Clancy walked down to the pub. He would miss these morning walks with the dew still on the grass and the slight mist in the air.

He went in and walked over to the bar, ordered a pint and then looked around. He spied Doc Flannery coming out of the men's toilet and walked over for a little chat.

Seeing him, Doc Flannery asked. "How is your arthritis? Any better?"

"I'm doing what you recommended."

"How's your investigation coming along?" He took a long sip of his drink. "I'm curious."

"Let's put it this way, I have a little scenario to tell you. You might find it interesting. The killing of Sister Gertrude was a spur of the moment action. The killer was presented with an opportunity, the opening of hunting season. Like most people in these parts, he no doubt kept a hunting rifle in the trunk of his car. He heard Sister Gertrude announce she was going to find the Mass Rock near the woodlot.

"A red Volkswagen was seen leaving the parking lot at The Crossroads mid-afternoon, just after Sister Gertrude announced her intentions of going to look for the rock. I believe it was the same car travelling on the concession road north of the woodlot later.

"We have the bullet that killed Sister Gertrude, but we don't have the gun. The weapon, a hunting rifle, is missing. Many farmers have guns for hunting. Do you go hunting, Doc?" asked Clancy.

"In season," he replied softly.

"May I enquire as to where your gun is at this moment?"

Dr. Flannery stared at him. "This may surprise you, but I regret to inform you that it was stolen several months ago from the trunk of my car."

"Did you file a police report?"

"I phoned the Gardai, but I didn't have the time to make a written submission. It was an old gun and I hardly ever used it. It

146

was of value to no one."

"So, it's very unlikely we'll ever find the gun again, to your way of thinking?"

Doc Flannery nodded. "You don't think my gun was used to kill Sister Gertrude, do you?" Doc Flannery leveled his deep blue eyes on Clancy.

"Ballistic tests would tell us if the bullet that came from that gun was the one that killed Sister Gertrude. But no gun, no tests. That's my little scenario for what its worth. No witnesses, just one bullet and a gun that has disappeared. Not much to go on. I leave for Canada in a few days."

"That's your story," said Doc Flannery, "and you have no evidence to back any of it up. What a shame. In my mind it's pretty thin and pretty libelous. I'll sue if anyone tries to blacken my name. Things are done differently over here. The Gardai don't go on fishing expeditions, just hard evidence." He went over to the bar and slammed his glass down.

Clancy shrugged his shoulders. "It's only a story, there's no evidence. Everything else is coincidental. "I've done the best I can do under the circumstances and the short amount of time given me." said Clancy, calmly sipping his beer. "I've finished my work and will soon depart. Surprisingly my hunches are usually right. Any last thoughts, Doc Flannery?"

"Libelous thoughts, dangerous thoughts. Perhaps, in future, you should stick to your sleuthing in Canada. You're stirring up nothing but trouble over here. Sister Gertrude was a blight on the landscape. Whoever did it should get a medal, not be hounded and prosecuted. She didn't have a friend within the parish or within miles."

"I'm not handing out medals to the person who did this," said Clancy. "A murder is a murder. Justice has to be served. Good day to you." He tipped his cap to Doc Flannery, turned and walked out of the bar.

**

Back at the Squire's, Clancy contacted Sergeant Feeney of the Gardai.

"It's Clancy here. I've had a wonderful visit in Ireland and was treated most generously. My plane leaves in three days, I just have to wind things up. I'm phoning to tell you my conclusion, although you may not agree with me. "My suspicions fall on Doc

Flannery."

"Him? Are you serious? That old coot. He's harmless." exclaimed Sergeant Finney

"Maybe. What have you heard about him?"

"Sister Gertrude was always coming to us, claiming that he did abortions and practiced euthanasia. It was all nonsense. There was never any evidence that we could find. We never charged him."

"That's the point. He wanted to shut her up once and for all."

"Tell me, Clancy, why you're sure it was him?"

"A red Volkswagen was seen leaving the pub shortly after Sister Gertrude announced that she was going to locate the Mass Rock. Another witness said he saw the same colour and make of that car mid afternoon on the back road behind the woodlot. No one got the license plate. Doc Flannery was in the pub that afternoon and he drives a red Volkswagen.

"As to the weapon, the hunting rifle, Doc Flannery claims his rifle was stolen from the trunk of his car several months ago. Who stole it? Will we ever find it?"

Sergeant Finney said, "We can keep looking for the rifle, but the chances of finding it are very slim. It's all circumstantial and too flimsy. It would be hard to prosecute. The defense would tear it apart. So would the judge. You need a witness to say, 'Doc went into the woodlot that afternoon'. You need a license number for the car and you haven't got one."

"Well, that's the best I can do."

"Thank you, Clancy. Publicly, to the press, we can say the case is open and ongoing. In the meantime, we'll keep an eye on Doc Flannery."

Clancy walked back into the library and was keeping the Squire company when there was a knock on the library door. Mansbridge announced, that Mr. Hunter, the archeologist from Trinity College, Dublin, was back and had some important news.

Beaming and excited, Mr. Hunter entered the room, put down his backpack and walking stick, nodded at the Squire and Clancy. "I bring you good news." he said, enthusiastically. "The Archeological Society of Ireland want to take a look at your rock. They're thinking of doing a survey and looking for artifacts. They think it is a Mass Rock like the others found in Cork County."

"Well, I have bad news for you," said the Squire, giving him a hard look. "There have been too many bad things happen there. First, my nephew met an accidental death in the woodlot and, just recently, a nun had her head blown off by a hunter down at the rock.

There's been nothing but evil associated with that, so called, Mass Rock."

"A nun was murdered? How awful. Did they catch the murderer?"

"Not yet. Too soon. There are too many suspects. I don't want people tramping through my property. I'm a private person and this is private property."

"But this is greater than ourselves. This is an historic artifact. This is looking at the past. These are sacred places which need to be protected and preserved for future generations. I hope you'll think ahead to future generations," said Mr. Hunter, vehemently."

"I can't help you there," replied the Squire.

"How can I persuade you to change your mind?"

"You can't. This is my final word on the matter."

"Well I'm very, very disappointed at your answer. I went to all the trouble of getting the Archeological Society all fired up and keen to do a survey. However, if that's your final word, then I'll be off." The archeologist picked up his walking stick and backpack from the chair and walked out.

"That's the end of that," said the Squire. "Let's have a toast to a peaceful future. Mansbridge, bring out the sherry."

Chapter 23

Two days later, Clancy popped into the duty-free shop and bought Agnes some expensive perfume and a bottle of gin as a peace offering before boarding his flight back to Toronto.

Again, he had a wonderful time in business class, accepting all the free drinks going. Hardly sober, but pretending to be, he passed through customs. What had he to declare? "Nothing," he said, "only a four-leaf clover." He had forgotten about the perfume and the gin.

Agnes had driven to pick him up at Pearson International, and was now standing outside the EXIT door. She warmly embraced him and gave him a big welcoming peck on the cheek. "It's great to have you back, dear. I missed you, the dog missed you and everyone missed you. I hope you brought me back something nice."

"Of course, Agnes."

They walked out to the parking building and got into the car to go home to Mariposa. From the back seat, Jack, the Jack Russell terrier barked, wagged his tail excitedly and gave him big slobbering tongue licks on the back of his neck. What an affectionate dog! Then Clancy heard a stream of water. He turned around. Jack had pissed onto the back seat of the car. "Oh migawd," thought Clancy, "I own a dog who has no control of its bladder."

"In my purse, which I can't reach while I'm driving," said Agnes, making pleasant conversation," I want to bring you up to scratch on what has been going on. I made a list of things we have to get done around the house. One of them is cleaning the leaves out of the eaves troughs before winter sets in."

"Oh, migawd," thought Clancy. He recalled the rickety ladder he used to do this in his younger days and pictured it falling over and killing him. He'd hire somebody, some teenager, who was younger and more fit to do it.

"It'll have to wait until I recover from jet lag, it'll take about a week." How he wished he was back at the Manor house, being waited on hand and foot, without a care in the world. In Ireland, he'd been spoiled rotten. Life in Mariposa was going to take some getting used to again. There would be chores and more chores and it would be hard to cook up enough excuses to duck any of them.

***

The next morning Clancy slept in, then got up, shaved, had a breakfast of scrambled eggs, toast and coffee, drank a second cup of coffee to try to shake off his jet lag, brushed his teeth and kissed Agnes goodbye. He staggered into the office late, at 10 a.m., sat down at his desk, chewed briefly on the end of his ballpoint, then tried to pull a thick black hair from the back of his hand.

Oh, but how boring it was to be back.

"So, the prodigal son returns, kill the fatted calf," said Greg, coming into the room.

"Getting Biblical on us, are we? Huh? Miss me? Couldn't get along without me?"

"Are you kidding? There's been no action. No murders, just a few B & Es. It's been like a tomb around here. Even that old lady, that friend of yours who lost her valuable cameo broach, has stopped popping in. What a pest. I was glad to see the last of her. And the red shirt anarchist, who walked his dog by every morning and let the dog foul our fire hydrant, has chosen a different morning route.

"You know that the murderer of your cousin in Toronto has been caught, using the footage from the security cameras and the carding system to search the police data bank for his name and address. It was a twenty-five-year-old Jamaican who lived in the Jane/Finch area. I don't know what the Toronto police will do if they get rid of the carding system."

"What would I do without you, Greg? I have a slight headache. Would it be too much trouble for you to go out and get some nice, fresh hot coffee at Apple Annie's and a big sugary doughnut?"

"I will if you're paying?" said Greg.

"Well, yes, of course I'll pay, just this once, seeing I have

152

been on vacation."

Clancy looked around the office. David was out on an investigation and had left a message on his answering machine, *'Great to have you back.'*

Greg set out to Apple Annie's for the coffee.

Now, thought Clancy, would be a good time to call Eli Brown, Mary Murphy's lawyer down in Toronto.

First, his secretary answered and then he was put through. "Hi, checking in. I just got back from Ireland."

"I've been meaning to call you. How was your trip?" asked the lawyer.

"Very pleasant. I stayed with Squire Murphy at the Manor House."

"How long were you gone?"

"Almost three weeks, a lot longer than I intended. The murder of a nun took place very near to where I was staying. The Gardai asked for my help. They were short staffed."

"That sounds intriguing."

"Yes and no. Not too much evidence was found. The Gardai are going to proceed on my recommendations."

"That's good to hear. You've fulfilled the conditions of the will and I can happily put the cheque in the mail to you. Do you think Ms. Murphy wanted you there to have a little snoop around? I think so. She was crazy about that nephew of hers who had that deadly accident. Did you come to any conclusions at all about that?"

"I came to the conclusion that Quincy, the youngest nephew, was a dangerous person to know and to have around. I had a pitchfork thrown in my direction, just narrowly missing me in the barn. I believe that it was Quincy who threw it. I warned the Squire about him. Hopefully he will take my advice."

"Well, you're back safe and sound. I'll put the cheque in the mail today."

"Thank you."

It will be nice, thought Clancy, to have spending money in my pocket, a gift that the government can't grab. Now to think of the many ways I can spend it.

Clancy's quiet reverie was suddenly interrupted by the front office door banging open. Mira blew in, tall black leather boots, leather motorcycle jacket and black leather mini skirt. She looked liked she'd just hopped off a motorcycle. She plopped herself down on a chair in front of his desk without asking permission. But did Mira ever ask for permission? Remind me, thought Clancy, to get rid of that chair. She crossed and uncrossed her legs so that Clancy could get a good view of England, Ireland, Scotland and France.

"Hello stranger, what's up? Hanging out with the toffs in a Manor house with servants waiting on you. Isn't that a bit rich for the likes of you? How does it feel to come back to earth and plant your feet on the ground?"

"Oh, Mira, I had to do an investigation while I was there. I really wasn't on holiday."

"You mean that murdered nun? Did she get lucky before she went to the pearly gates? Tell me about it."

"It wasn't easy. A lot of people disliked her. She had a lot of enemies in the village. But I fingered one person, the local doctor, whom she was trying to get put in jail for what she claimed was practicing abortion and euthanasia, as the one who pulled the trigger. He had the most to lose, but finding witnesses and evidence was a bit difficult. He claimed that his hunting rifle was stolen from the trunk of his car, which means no gun, no matching bullets, no evidence. I told the Gardai my findings and they're going to carry on the investigation. Hopefully they will find some evidence to get a conviction."

"So, it has not all gone to waste," said Mira, drumming her scarlet nails rat, a-tat-tat, on the wooden desk.

"Nothing is wasted ever, Mira," said Clancy, firmly. "Investigations take time, especially if the prosecution is going to get a successful guilty verdict. Some cold cases go on for years, but eventually they get solved. A good copper never gives up."

"Ah nuts, justice has been served already. The obnoxious nun was gotten rid of. Somebody deserves a medal, not an arrest. Get real."

"Mira, we don't live in anarchy where people mete out their special brand of justice. It has to be fair and square. Justice has to be served."

"Crap," said Mira again. "Anyway, are you glad to be back here with us peasants?"

"It's good to be home," said Clancy, which was a bit of a lie, but never the less good for public relations value. "I've still got jet lag. Where I came from it's already two in the afternoon but it's always good to get away to recharge my batteries and come back with a fresh perspective."

"What a load of bullshit," said Mira, getting up from her chair and preparing to leave, knocking some of his papers onto the floor. "You don't fool me. You wish you were back in that Manor house with the butler waiting on you hand and foot."

Clancy sighed, if only life were that simple. He settled back in his chair to look at the piled-up paperwork, a list marked 'urgent' on top of his memos. He heard a timid knock on the door. "Come in," he roared. A little girl, ten years old, with long blonde hair and blue eyes, in a pink t- shirt, sweatpants and running shoes was holding to her chest a big black rabbit.

"Who are you? "asked Clancy

"I'm Claire, I'm ten years old and this is my rabbit. I thought you might like to see it. I took it to the fall fair and talked to the judge about how I am caring for my rabbit." She plopped the big rabbit with the twitching nose down on the memo pile on his desk.

"I feed my rabbit romaine lettuce, potato skins and carrots. Today I made a salad for my rabbits of banana and carrots. I didn't win a prize for that, but I won several other prizes. With the prize money, I bought another rabbit, but I can't carry both in to show you."

Clancy looked at the rabbit, the rabbit looked at him, made a little noise, a little cloud of vapour went up and then a nice warm pile of grey pellets dropped out of its rear end and onto his urgent memos.

"Shit," thought Clancy "and it's ones that I haven't even read yet." He grimaced.

"Sorry," said Claire, peering at the pile, "rabbits do that every so often. Do you want me to help you clean it up?"

"Thanks, Claire, that was a nice visit. Thanks for coming by. I think it best to keep the rabbit in its cage. They get nervous around people."

Without saying a word, Claire collected the rabbit up in her arms and left. She looked deeply offended

"Shit, shit, and more shit," said Clancy. "On my memos and I haven't even read them yet. My first day back. Re-entry is worse than I thought."

Epilogue

Three months later, on a crisp cold January morning when Jack Frost had, overnight, coated all the tree branches with snow and ice, when the roads were slippery causing traffic accidents, and everything was bleak and forlorn, when the salt trucks had been out on the roads all night and the sidewalks were covered in sand and salt—salt which could discolour your leather boots—when the glow of Christmas had passed and the Three Wise Men had come and gone, Clancy sat in his office and watched the wet snow pelting down. He'd turned the heat up full blast. David was out getting snow tires put on his car. He'd left it rather late in the season to do this. Not smart, not planning ahead. Greg was looking at photos of break-ins turning them over one by one, so bored he could hardly keep awake. He wanted to fall asleep and hibernate like every black bear in Simcoe county, but Clancy, the boss, was back and he'd better look busy. He sighed. Things were slow as molasses.

Clancy heard a gentle knock on the front door. He opened it cautiously to keep out the blowing wind and freezing snow. He looked down at a small figure in black.

A scratchy, timid voice said. "May I come in for a glass of water? I hate to ask you for this favour. I know this isn't the place to ask for that."

Clancy looked at her. She reminded him of his mother, this little figure dressed in a black hat with a felt brim and feather and wearing a black overcoat with a fur collar covered in wet snowflakes.

"I was on my way to the pharmacy to get some digitalis tablets for my angina. I need to stop in here and catch my breath."

"Here, come in here, my dear," said Clancy "You sit right

down on this chair and get warm. I'll go and get you some water. Are you sure you wouldn't like a nice cup of hot coffee?"

"Very sure. Water will be just fine."

Clancy brought her the water. "Sit here until you feel able to go out again. It's a nasty day. You shouldn't be out on a day like this."

"You are so kind," murmured the old lady. "Normally I wouldn't but I 've run out of pills. I get angina. If I don't take them. I have an attack. They prevent me from dying." She put a gloved hand to her heart.

The old lady sat quietly in the chair sipping the water. Clancy glanced over at her from time to time, to make sure she was alright, while he attempted to do some paperwork. Twenty minutes passed. Was her heart still fluttering? She got up to go.

"Are you sure you can walk home?" asked Clancy. "I can send you back to your place in a patrol car. It'll be a lot safer and faster than walking."

"I don't mind. I just have to climb the small hill up Peter Street, past the Presbyterian Church. I don't want to be any trouble. I don't want to be a burden on anyone. You've been so very kind. God bless you."

Clancy let her out and closed the door. It was fierce outside with the wind and snow blowing in all directions. He was glad that he wasn't out there. Deep in his heart he had a nice, warm feeling for letting the old lady have a rest. He had doubts about her making it up the hill without breaking a leg on the black ice, but some old ladies are like tigers, fierce and determined. Nothing stops them. If they want to do something, they will.

He settled back in his chair, and let his thoughts take him back to Ireland, to Tricia, to the Squire and the Manor House. He thought about The Crossroads where he had spent many happy hours in front of the fire. Being warmed by the Gulf Stream, they wouldn't have weather like this over there. At Christmas, the Squire had sent a greeting card, very formal, with a comment that he hoped that he would find his way over there again.

He thought of that Irish hottie, Tricia, with the melon like knockers and the broad behind whom he had never quite got his hands on. He remembered her zipping down country lanes in a mad dash. Would she miss him as much as he missed her? He thought of her patient, Paddy Johnson, who couldn't keep his pajamas tied up around his waist.

Tricia had sent him a nice Christmas card, signed with fond

wishes. In her remarks she'd said that they were all well, but they missed him at the pub. The owner, Liam Cross, often asked if she'd heard from him. She was glad to tell him that Sabrina had broken off her relationship with Quincy - she was getting too many bruises which couldn't be explained away. Quincy, she heard, had been banned from the Squire's house and no longer worked for him. His whereabouts, at the moment, were unknown. He was a really bad egg. It was nice to hear her news, but not as good as being there.

Clancy decided to check his email on his computer. An email from Father Flynn? Didn't expect to find this. Clancy pressed open.

Greetings. I hope this letter finds you happy and well over the Christmas season that has just past. People here are asking for you. We raised a toast to you in the pub. We miss you and hope someday you will find time to return to see us. The reason for my writing is that I write with a heavy heart. It is to inform you of the sad news that our friend, Doc Flannery, has gone from this life to his eternal rest. You knew that he was quite ill when you were over here visiting His oncologist in Dublin said that all he could offer him at this late stage was for him to enter palliative care. There was nothing more he could do for him. He had run out of options.

Doc Flannery entered palliative care two weeks ago. He was in great pain. The medical staff did their best to alleviate it. I went up to Dublin several times to visit him. On his deathbed, I performed the sacrament of the sick, making the sign of the cross, anointing his forehead, chest and hands with Holy Oil. Before Vatican Two, this was known as extreme unction (unctio in extremis) but now is given to those that are seriously ill along with those that are dying.

He confessed to the murder of Sister Gertrude. It had been an accident, he said. After she left the pub and said she was going to the woodlot to find the Mass Rock by the stream, he drove up there on the north concession, then took the path into the woods to the clearing. He finally found her standing by the Mass Rock. They got into an argument. He told her that he was tired of being libeled by her remarks that he was committing criminal acts such as abortion and euthanasia in the parish and surrounding country-side. He threatened her. He wanted her to stop. To emphasize his point, he slammed the hunting rifle's butt on the ground. His shot gun discharged accidentally killing her instantly. He did not mean to kill her, he said, he had only meant to threaten her. It was all a big mistake. Afterwards, he drove to Cork, walked along the cliffs and threw his hunting rifle into the Irish Sea.

Even though she was an unpleasant woman, he had never meant to kill her. It all had been a big accident. He said that several times.

I knew you had been asked by the Gardai to help in the investigation to find the murderer of Sister Gertrude. You can forward my email to the Gardai. I don't think I am violating any trust. Doc Flannery is gone from this life. If it were not a murder investigation, I would not volunteer this information. A death bed confession is sacred.

Peace be with you and yours,

Father Flynn.

"The Gardai can now close the book on that one," thought Clancy, "and I can too. My intuition was right all along. Although it is a sad ending, at least it saves the public the expense of a long trial and the public humiliation of Doc Flannery. He must have been desperate to shut her up. Justice has been served. As Shakespeare said, all's well that ends well."

www.ingramcontent.com/pod-product-compliance
Lightning Source LLC
Chambersburg PA
CBHW052139170626
46812CB00004B/1505

* 9 7 8 0 9 9 3 9 9 7 9 4 5 *